Dedications

This book 'Luath, Clarinda and The Redwood Tree' is dedicated to John Shirreffs and Frankie Allen, two good friends who are sadly missed, and also to my late aunt Margaret Connacher and to my son Matthew, whose mother will one day see the light.

Special thanks to Rena, Lynsey, and all friends who helped me with this book, and to my brother George for the front cover sketch of Robert Burns.

Introduction

On the night of 'oor Rabbie's' birthday, 25th of January 1996, two wee boys, Grant Forrest and Grant Hendrie chapped on my door because they had found a wee dog running about in the snow, and were looking for a home for it. Two days later I found out that the wee pup belonged to a Mr Johnstone who was delighted to have him returned safe and well. But I was a wee bit sorry to hand him over.

Most of the events in this tale are true.

**A Crambo Clinker is a Rhymer*

Redwood Tree

The Redwood provides the tallest and possibly the most majestic tree in the world. It grows to a height of almost 400 feet, and lives up to two thousand years. The native habitat of the tree, is a strip of land some thirty miles wide stretching from about one hundred miles south of San Francisco to Southwest Oregon. The Redwood (Sequoia) honours a famous half-bred Cherokee chief, Sequoia. The tree was introduced to Britain via Russia in 1843.

The song, Redwood Tree was written by Van Morrison and can be found on his album St. Dominic's Preview. This song gave me some of the inspiration to write this wee story, if you ever get a chance to listen to it, do so, you will never be the same, it's brilliant.

It is also said that the Redwood Tree has great mystical powers.

Luath, Clarinda and The Redwood Tree

Chapter 1

A wee pup falls from heaven

It was the year of Our Lord 1996 in Auld Campsie Toun, on the evening of the 25th of January, the birthday of Robert Burns, Scotland's greatest son. The Bard was renowned throughout the world, from Mauchline to Murmansk and Helensburgh to Hawaii. The legend lives on forever.

Auld Jock lifted his penny-wheep (small beer) and toasted the Bard.
"Cheers Rabbie, awe the best, if you were alive today you would be two hundred and thirty seven years old, God bless you." A silly thought, thocht Jock, but the way technology was going it would not be long till people would be living to that age.
"Ach Rabbie ye wir born too early son, what a politician you would have made, for awe that n' awe that." Jock lifted up the poker and broke up the lumpy coal on the fire and returned to his book. The book by James Barke, 'The Wind That Shakes The Barley', was about the life and times of Robert Burns. Jock was engrossed in every page, it was as if he was there, transferred back in time, brilliant.

The book was a gift from his daughter Maggie, along with another four books by the same author, also about the Bard. The others were.

'The Song In The Greenthorn Tree'
'The Wonder Of All The Gay World'
'The Crest Of The Broken Wave' and
'The Well Of The Silent Harp.' First class reading!

Twenty minutes later Jock had drifted into the arms of the Sandman. The heat of the fire and his auld eyes had given in and he was sleeping like a wee baby. Half an hour later he awoke to find that the fire had died down, so he stretched his arms and got up and went to the coal bunker. There he got a log and a shovel of dross and put them on the fire. He put the fireguard up against the fire and lifted his book. He thought to himself, 'aye the watter will be lovely and warm in the mornin' for a guid bath.'

Later on he went over to the front window and keeked (spied) through the curtains, this was a ritual Jock had performed every night for years. 'What a night' Jock thought. The snow was getting thicker and must have been about ten inches deep. 'A widny put a milk bottle oot on a night like that.' Jock laughed to himself.

As he walked to the bedroom he heard somebody at the door, bang, bang, bang. 'Who in God's name's that at this time of night?' He thought. He looked at the clock, it was nine o' clock. He shouted from behind the door.
"Who's that?"
"It's Jamie and Megan Pappa."
Jock opened the door, and there stood his two grandchildren covered in snow.

"Whit in God's name are yees doin' oot oan a night like this, give yirselves a shake an come awa in and get a heat."
The children went in and Jock closed the door and turned round. Megan said.
"Look what we found Pappa runnin' aboot in the snaw."
From under her coat Megan produced a wee puppy.
"Oh my God, where did yees find him?"
"We found him Pappa honest, joost alang the road, the poor wee thing is frozen." Said Jamie.
"Well quick take him into the fireplace."

Jock went and got a bath towel and started to dry the wee puppy.
"I wonder whose puppy he is Pappa, there will be people out looking for him, just as well we were out having a snowball fight or he might have died." Said Megan.
"Probably Megan, or maybe they think he's dead or maybe they don't care, or maybe somebody got him for Xmas and couldn't care less about the wee thing. Anyway he's here now so joost get him dried and keep him warm, I'll go and get him some hot milk and something to eat."

"How do you know he's a he Pappa?"
"Well let's have a look, aye he's a boy alright, and he ain't no tyke (mongrel) either, he's a border collie, sure enough." Said Jock.
"Can we keep him Pappa?"
"Oh no Jamie we can't, he doesn't belong to us. We will have to find out who he belongs to and take him back."

Jock 'phoned up his daughter Maggie and told her what had happened. The kids were allowed to stay the night and sleep on Jock's bedcouch, if he would bring them round in the morning.

A wee while later as Jock was lying in bed, he thought. 'What an unbelievable coincidence, a border collie lands on my doorstep on the night of Robert Burns birthday. It was as if it was meant to happen, sent to him from heaven.' But he knew the puppy had to belong to someone, and the kids would be disappointed when they found the owner.

The following morning Jock woke to the sound of a wee pup yelping. Yelp, yelp yelp. He quickly got dressed and went in to the living room, where Megan and Jamie were playing on top of the bed with the puppy.
"What's all the noise, about?" Oh no! Jock had stood in a wee puddle. He grabbed the wee puppy by the scruff of the neck and dipped it's nose in the puddle and gave him a wee skelp(slap).
"Bad puppy." Said Jock. He carried the puppy to the back door and put him out in the snow.
"That's cruel." Said Megan.
"It's not cruel, he will have to be house trained, and that's the only way to do it, it's for his own good."
"Can we keep him Pappa, please can we?" Asked Jamie.
"No I told you, we would have to find out if he's been reported missing, then we will see what happens."
Secretly Jock hoped that they would never find the owner, but he couldn'y tell the kids that.
"Now get yir claes oan, I'll get the pup in and light the fire."

Twenty minutes later Jock had made the breakfast. He walked into the living room with a huge tray, and on the tray were three large soup plates, full and piping hot. But it was not soup and it was not porridge. Jock placed the plates on the big table along with some bread and butter.
"What's that Pappa?" Asked Megan.
"That's mince and poached eggs, get in tae it, it's lovely."

The kids were a bit sceptical at first, but once they tasted it and started dooking in the bread they weren't long in devouring the lot.
"That was brill Pappa, is there any more?" Said Jamie.
"Aye, smashin' Pappa, can I give some to the puppy?" Megan said.
"There's a wee drop left in the pot for him."

Five minutes later as they stood in the scullery (kitchen) watching the wee pup eat. Jock said.
"Look at that white mark on the crown of his head, it looks like the Star of David."
"So it does Pappa, that's amazing!"

And so Jock, Megan and Jamie and the wee pup all went back into the living room. Jock told the kids to settle down and he would show them a video. The fire was roaring and everything was nice and cosy. Outside the snow was still falling and the traffic was at a standstill. Jock looked over at Jamie and Megan lying on the bedcouch with the wee pup. A wee tear came to his eye as he thought, 'they weans are gonny be heartbroken when that pup goes back to it's owner.'

Chapter Two

A Wee Dog Gets A Name

The house was covered in snow as the Range Rover pulled out of the driveway. It was about the only vehicle, which could move, in the terrible conditions. The owner of the Rover was Dr Henson, and he had just been to see young Clarinda Brady who was very ill. Clarinda was suffering from a serious kidney condition and Dr Henson had told her parents that she would have to go back into Yorkhill Children's Hospital for more tests. The ambulance was due to pick Clarinda up that morning.

Five minutes later Mr Brady was walking into his bedroom when he suddenly remembered the wee pup that he had bought for Clarinda. He was so upset that he had forgotten all about it. It was supposed to be a surprise. He just couldn't understand how it got out of the house. Clarinda hadn't even seen the poor wee thing. And there's no way it would have survived last nights snowstorm. He walked over to the window and started to wipe the condensation from the windowpanes.

About a couple of hundred yards away he could see two small figures playing in the snow with what looked like a wee puppy. 'It can't be, he thought.' He ran down the stairs and told his wife what he had seen. A few minutes later Mr Brady was about thirty yards from the two kids and the wee pup. He stood and watched them for a couple of minutes. They were so happy that a sadness came over Mr Brady as he watched them playing with the pup. 'That should be Clarinda playing out there he thought.'

But for some strange reason he was also happy inside. He walked over to the kids and said.
"Hi kids, that's a lovely wee puppy you have there, where did you get him?" He knew that the puppy was the one he had bought for Clarinda, but he didn't have the heart to tell them.
Well, Jamie and Megan were told never to tell lies, and they were not going to start now.
"We found him last night Mr Brady, he was lost in the snow." Said Megan.
Mr Brady admired the children's honesty; all he said was.
"Is your Pappa in the house?"
"Yes Mr Brady, he's making a big pot of soup."

Five minutes later Jock and Mr Brady were sitting at the coal fire. Jock had poured John Brady a dram of malt whisky.
"Cheers Jock." Said John.
"Awe the best John, I knew your father well he was a good man."

"Thanks Jock, he always spoke highly of you, it's a real pleasure to meet you."
John told Jock all about Clarinda.

"Ach that's a shame John, we'll all say some prayers for her at Mass on Sunday."
Then he told Jock about the puppy.
"Aye it's lucky the kids were out last night or the poor wee thing would have been dead."
"Well Jock, I had actually bought the pup for Clarinda's birthday, she doesn't even know, poor soul."
"Ach well, I'll go and tell Megan and Jamie to bring him in."
"No Jock, the wee pup's in very good hands, and I've never seen children so happy. They can keep him. Do you want to shout them in and I'll tell them?"
"I certainly will John, that's very generous of you; they'll be the happiest kids in the world."

Two minutes later Megan said.
"Oh thanks very much Mr Brady, we will look after him and give him plenty of love and take him for long walks, eh Jamie?"
"Aye, we love him Mr Brady." Said Jamie.
"What's his name, Mr Brady?"
"Well we only got him last night, we've not had a chance to give him a name."
"There's only one name you can give that pup." Said Jock.
"What's that Pappa?" Said Megan.
"Yesterday was Robert Burns's birthday, and he had a border collie called Luath, so you must call him Luath. This was meant to happen, it's fate."
"That's a lovely name Jock, Luath it is then. Well I've got to go, Clarinda's going into the hospital."
"Can we go and visit Clarinda Mr Brady?"
"Of course you can Megan, she would love that."

And so it was later on that night that Jock began to think. 'What a strange life this is. A wee pup landed on his doorstep, a Border collie tae, on the night of the Bard's birthday, what a weird coincidence. A mans wee girl gets taken into hospital, and the Border collie belongs to that wee girl, but her Daddy has given the pup to a wee boy and a wee girl, and they are so happy, strange indeed.'
Then Jock remembered what John F Kennedy had said many years ago.
"Anybody who says that life is fair has been seriously misinformed."

Later on that day Maggie, Megan and Jamie's mother arrived at Jock's. When she opened the door she could smell the homemade soup wafting down the hallway. As she entered the living room Luath ran over to her.

"Hi kids, hi Dad." She started to clap Luath. "Oh my, isn't he gorgeous? That was very good of Mr Brady to give the pup to you. It's a shame about Clarinda though."
"Aye Mum it's terrible, we've to go into the Yorkhill Hospital to visit her. Luath was sitting on Maggie's lap, and she was getting very fond of the new addition to her family.

Jamie said. "Mum can we stay at Pappa's again tonight, cos the school will still be closed because of the snow?"
"That's up to your Pappa." Said Maggie.
"Nae problem, of course you can stay. We will be going for a wee daunder (walk) later with Luath. But before that we are gonny have some broth, it's ready, so awa' and wash yir Frankie Vaughns (hauns, hands)."
So the kids raced down the hall into the toilet, followed by Luath. As they washed their hands Luath was yelping, he was happy, for he knew something good was going to happen, he was going to be fed.

While the kids were in the toilet Jock said to Maggie.
"I will keep Luath here until he is house trained, so you don't have to clean up his mess in the morning."
"Aye, thanks Dad, that's a relief."
"Maybe later on this week once the snow clears we'll take the kids in to see Clarinda, will you drive us in Maggie?"
"Aye certainly Dad that would be nice."

Five minutes later they were all sitting at Jock's big table enjoying the home made soup, with the big lumps of ham. Jock put some soup mixed with bread down for Luath, but he could not eat it because it was too warm. Jamie shouted to Luath.
"Blow on it Luath, blow on it."
"Don't be daft Jamie, a dog doesn't know how to blow." Said Megan.

Chapter 3

The Snow on the River

Jock and the kids were walking along the auld railway, the snow was about ten inches deep, and there were huge drifts all over the place. Jock said.
"Do you know what used to be here, what this path used to be?"
"No, what was it Pappa?"
"The steam trains used to run up here, this is the auld railway line, they used to pass under this bridge."
"How long ago was that Pappa?" Asked Megan.
"They stopped running in the early nineteen sixties, I used to work on them. When I stayed down at the (Tar-Row), Rowantree Terrace, I would get up at half past four in the morning, get on my bike and cycle into Glasgow."
"In to Glasgow, that's amazing Pappa." Jamie said.

"Aye, there we would get the train ready and leave for Aberfoyle. We would pass through Kirkintilloch, Milton of Campsie, Lennoxtown and then Blanefield, picking up passengers, parcels, mail and goods all the way up to Aberfoyle, and the same on the way back."
"But how did you get back to work the next day Pappa?" Asked Megan, who was a good listener.
"Aye yir no daft Megan, how do you think I got back?"
"You must have taken the bike on the train Pappa, because you told me before that you always got off at the Tar-Row every night."
"That's right Megan, you've got a good memory." Said Jock.

They walked on, and soon they came to a wee path, which ran down to the banks of the river Glazert, and there stood the big Redwood Tree. Jock walked over to the tree and put his arms around it. He said to the children.
"C'mon over kids and say hello, and give the tree a wee cuddle."
Megan and Jamie walked over to the tree and gave it a cuddle; somehow they knew that it was a natural thing to do. Jock said.
"Why do you think I asked you to cuddle the tree?"
"Don't know Pappa." They both said.
"Because that tree is a living thing, that tree is growing right now, and the Redwood Tree is a mystical tree. It's named after a Cherokee Indian called Sequoyah, and it's supposed to have magical powers."
"What age is it Pappa?' Asked Jamie.

“Well that tree must be about 160 years old. There are actually giant Redwoods in California that are over two thousand years old. There are pictures of cars driving through the middle of them.”
“They must be some size Pappa.” Said Jamie.
“Aye, they grow up to four hundred feet tall, they’re fantastic.”

The snow started to fall again, mixed with drops of rain. Jock said.
“Look at the snow falling on the river.” Suddenly Jock remembered a verse from the poem ‘Tam O’ Shanter’, by Robert Burns, and quoted.

“But pleasures are like poppies spread,
You seize the flow’r, its bloom is spread,
Or like the snow falls on the river,
A moment white then melts forever.”

“That’s a wee quote from ‘Tam O’Shanter’ one of Burns poems. Just watch the snow as it lands on the water.”
“It just disappears Pappa, gone forever.” Said Megan.
“Aye, I think we better start back home kids, c’mon Luath.”

“I’m learning a Burns poem at school Pappa.” Said Megan.
“What’s it called?”
“My Love is Like a Red Red Rose.”
“That’s great Megan, can you quote it to me?” Said Jock. Megan laughed and said.
“Once I learn it all by heart Pappa, you will be the first to hear it.”
“Great, now let’s get moving, that snow is getting heavier, c’mon.”

And so they headed back home. The snowflakes were getting bigger and wee Luath was beginning to struggle. So Jock lifted him up and tucked him under his coat. Megan and Jamie looked up at Luath and their Pappa and just smiled, they were so happy, this was the greatest day of their lives.

About half an hour later they all sat down at Jock’s big table. They had soup again, followed by ham chips and beans. Then Megan and Jamie washed and dried the dishes, as their Pappa put logs and coal on the fire. Then they all sat down to watch a film ‘Lassie Come Home.’

Then out of the blue Megan says.
“Pappa, if Clarinda dies will she go to heaven?”
Jock was caught off guard, sometimes kids could ask some awkward questions.

“Och, don’t be daft Megan’, Clarinda will be fine, she’ll be able to go for walks with us once she gets out of hospital. Let’s just watch the film.”

“Do you think you’ll go to heaven Pappa?” Asked Jamie.

"Ach a don't know son, they'll probably let me in for half an hour, just to let me see what I've missed. Let's talk about heaven some other time; let's watch 'Lassie.'

Later that night before they all went to bed, they each said their prayers for Clarinda. Outside the snow had turned to rain, and every snowdrop had vanished. It seemed as if it was a message for the snowdrops underground to awaken and make everybody smile.

As Jock lay in bed reflecting on the day he thought. 'Aye it was a good day, it was nice to take the weans for a wee walk, and now that they had Luath there would be plenty more walks. He would take them up the Campsies, up the moors, the forestry, everywhere. He would teach them the history of Campsie. He would tell them how Rob Roy MacGregor came over the hills to steal the cattle, and about Benny Lynch, Scotland's greatest ever World champion boxer, aye and plenty more. But most of all he thought he would teach them honesty and integrity, never to tell lies and never to be selfish, because these were the things that were very important in the education of any child. And Luath would be trained to be a good dog and to be obedient. Aye it's been a good day, let's hope there's plenty more of them.'

The next morning Jock was making the breakfast while Megan and Jamie were cleaning up Luath's mess.
"Bad puppy." Said Megan, as she dipped Luath's nose in the wee puddle, and gave him a skelp.
"You've got to learn to do the toilet outside, right c'mon we're going for a wee walk before breakfast."
So off they went. Jock was laughing to himself as he thought. 'Aye they're learning, Luath will be house trained in no time.'

Ten minutes later the kids came back with Luath. Jamie said.
"That Luath ran away Pappa and we couldn'y catch him."
"What have I told you, you must keep him on the lead, otherwise he will not get trained properly. And it's also not fair on the dog, people get dogs and they don't train them the correct way, and guess what happens?"
"What?" Said Jamie.
"Well, the poor dog becomes disobedient and starts to run wild. Then the owner starts to hit the dog, but it's not the dogs' fault, it's the owners. The owners should actually hit themselves. It's the same with children; if they are not brought up properly they will be disobedient for the rest of their lives. Now get yir Frankie Vaughns washed, yir scrambled eggs and toast are ready."

A wee while later as they passed the big house where Clarinda lived. Megan said.
"Can we go into the hospital to see Clarinda, Pappa?"
"Aye we will be, your mother is taking us in on Sunday."
"Oh great Pappa, we'll buy her something nice." Said Jamie.

As they passed the big house they did not notice that a stranger had landed on the holly tree. His name was Robin Redbreast, where he came from nobody knew. Some mysterious force had guided him to the big house. And Robin Redbreast would be there for quite some time.

As they opened the door and walked into Maggies house, Jock shouted.
"Hi Maggie are you in, I've brought yir weans hame?"
"Hello there." Said Maggie. 'I thought you had moved into your Pappa's for good."
"Ach, they can stay with me anytime." Said Jock.
"Pappa can we come down in the morning and see Luath before going to school?" Asked Megan.
"Of course you can, and after school as well. And you can stay with me at the weekends until Luath is properly house trained. Then you will be able to take him to your own house."
"That's great Pappa." Said Jamie.
"Mum, are you definitely taking us in to see Clarinda on Sunday?"
"Oh yes Megan, I sure am."

A wee while later as Jock passed the big house he was thinking about Clarinda. 'Isn't life weird, there's wee Clarinda lying in the hospital not well, she comes from a good family, stays in a big house' no money problems, yet she hasn't got good health, a strange life indeed.' It reminded Jock of a wee girl that he once met coming back from a trip to the Canary Islands. She was with her Mum and Dad and Jock got talking to them. The wee girl was blind and deaf and could not speak, the poor wee soul. 'Ach.' Jock thought, 'we should all count our blessings; people don't know how lucky they are to have good health. What a strange and wonderful life it is.'

Chapter 4

Jock Goes to the Auld Hoose

As Jock entered the Auld Hoose he could see his auld drouthy cronie (thirsty friend) Duncan MacGregor sitting in the lounge by the blazing fire. Jock got the twa nappies (two beers) from the bar and sat down beside him.
"Aye, it's yirsel Jock, thanks for the beer, is this not the right place to be in on a night like it is?"
"You better believe it Duncan, the weather forecast is minus 9 tonight."
"Aye it's not a fit night out for man nor beast."
"That wind would cut right through you Duncan."

Auld Duncan who was eighty-six years old had been a friend of Jock's for over forty years, and knew all Jock's family. In fact auld Duncan knew everybody in the area, and everybody knew him. He was very well respected. And at eighty-six he was still a very fit and active man. He still walked five or six miles every day, come hail or shine, it was the walking he said that kept him fit. He also made his own meals, and would still have his two or three pints of beer every night, quite a man. He was also, so he claimed, a distant relative of Rob Roy MacGregor, and that's why he could walk a lot. Away back in those days the drovers could cover long distances, well, some of them had to.

Two or three pints later old Duncan suddenly remembered he had something to show Jock. He said.
"Ach Jock I'm sorry, ma auld memory is lettin' me doon. Have a read at that, it's unbelievable, that bit there, and the poem on the back."
The piece of paper was a newsletter from St Machan's Church in 1980.

History/Geography.

There are two ranges of hills in Campsie, which are of volcanic origin, namely the Fells and the South Braes. A strath or valley lies between these two hills, and it's from this strath that the name of Campsie or Campsi is derived. In the Celtic language it means 'Crooked Valley.'

May the Lord bless and protect you all.
Father William Forrester SJ and Father Mac.
And on the back of the newsletter was the following poem.

A Dream Of Home

'Neath it's Fells lies the village of Campsie,
And it's beauty is there to see,
The Crow Road, the Clachan, St Machans,
It's there that my heart longs to be.

The Glen down below has known millions,
That has trodden its beautiful grass,
And breathed in the air so refreshing,
Where time never seems to pass.

Where the Bard wrote verse of the Smiddy,
The Stansey behind the Glen burn,
Laird Kincaid Lennox, Rob Roy and his band,
And the heather clad slopes MacGregor commands.

And young Jamie Foyer made immortal in song,
St Machan, our son, brought heritage strong,
His church in the village, where his flock go to mass,
Ah! There's no place on earth could ever surpass.

The Holyknowe mound where he knelt in prayer,
And St Machan's Well still stands there,
The walk roon the moon, or away up the line,
Be it wet, stormy weather or ever so fine.

The clear Glazert burn or old Baker's Well,
The village serene can cast it's own spell,
The Taw Raw, the Main Street, the Kirk on the Hill,
The road to the Glen or Haughhead's Glenmill.

The Station Road, the Field Park below,
And the folk, O so kindly, that I use to know,
The Rod and Big Toshie, Moose and the Yat,
The Clincher, the Yoke, and old Stulty Pat.

And poachers wae dugs up on the mair,
To snare and catch a rabbit or hare,
Big Duncan McHardie, king o' the lot,
And many a rabbit we got for the pot.

The troot in the Glazert, the dyes in the lade,
It came from the 'Pheel' where the cloth it was made,
The fighting cocks of old Jock McCann,
McDuff, old Moshie and wee Flannagan.

Big Hairy Mary, and Muffin, Printer Neilie too,
The times were real hard with men on the Buroo,
Wee Pimple and Bud, Pistol forbye,
The real kindly neighbours bring a tear to the eye.

The hills and the Glen, dreams they will pass,
The bells of St Machan's still ring out for Mass,
I'll be there in spirit'o, God speed the day,
When I will return to my home in Campsie.

As auld Duncan sat down he said to Jock.
"What do you make of that Jock?"
"Aye, that's certainly a nice poem, but that bit about the geology of Campsie is a cracker. The Crooked Valley, it's well named."
"Ach don't be daft Jock, Campsie's joost like Ayr, full of honest men and bonnie lasses."
"All I can say Duncan is, whoever gave Campsie its name must have been able to see into the future."
"Aye, it's nice to know that you can go to bed at night and wake up in the morning and the roof is still attached to your house." Said Duncan, with a wry smile.
"Aye, and that bit at the end where Father Forrester says, 'May the Lord bless and protect you all,' nice one." Said Jock.

"Aye, and all the old characters in the poem, I remember the Rod used tae come oot the Burns Tavern full of the drink, and he would shout up the Graveyard hill to his mother who had been dead a few years." "Ach ye should see them noo Maw, way thir washin machines and thir fridges, they don't know how lucky they ur, we hud nothing."
"Aye he was some man the Rod." Said Jock.

Chapter 5

The Visit to Yorkhill Hospital

And so Sunday arrived and Maggie and the kids went to pick up Jock to drive him into Yorkhill Hospital. They stopped at a big supermarket in Bearsden and bought a big bunch of flowers and fruit for Clarinda. As they left the supermarket Maggie said to Jock.
"Dad have you heard anything about Clarinda?"
"Aye, I was talking to her Dad last night in the Auld Hoose, and it seems as though she is going to go on a dialysis machine."
"Poor wee soul." Maggie said.
"What's a Dallas machine?" Asked Jamie.
"Not a Dallas machine Jamie, a dialysis machine." Said Jock.
Jock and Maggie laughed.
"What's that?" Asked Megan.
"It's a machine that purifies the blood if your kidneys are not working properly, and makes you feel better."
"So this machine will make Clarinda better." Said Megan.
"Well, not really, she might still have to get a kidney transplant, we'll see, here's the Hospital now, we'll find out later." Said Jock. As they left the car Jamie said.
"We should have brought Luath in to see Clarinda."
"See you Jamie your daft, you don't bring dogs into hospitals." Said Megan.
"You see dogs on the telly in the hospital." Said Jamie.
"Och that's the Animal Hospital, this is a children's hospital." Said Megan.

Jock and Maggie were laughing at Jamie and Megan as they walked in the main entrance. The hospital was very busy, Jock said to Maggie.
"I didn'y realise there were so many sick children Maggie."
"Aye, there's plenty of them Dad, the work they do in here is absolutely brilliant. C'mon kids let's buy something for Clarinda from the Children's Fund shop, all the money goes to the kids." After they bought a couple of things for Clarinda they got the lift up to Ward 1C.

Clarinda was overjoyed to see them. They gave Clarinda her gifts and sat down and had a wee talk to her. Later Jock gave Maggie a wee nod to let the kids be alone with Clarinda. They moved outside the room and had a wee talk to the nurse.

“Oh he’s lovely Clarinda, he’s got a white star on the crown of his head, he’s gorgeous. And Pappa takes us for walks down to the Glazert to the big Redwood Tree, and when you are better you can come with walks with us.” Said Megan.
“That’s great Megan, the doctor says I will get home in a couple of days.”
“That’s great Clarinda, we’ll come round and see you with Luath.”
“Oh, that’s lovely Megan.”
“Well Clarinda, we’ll see you in a couple of days.”
“Bye.” Said Jamie.
“See you later.” Said Megan.
“Thanks for coming in, and thanks for the gifts.” Said Clarinda.

As Megan walked away from Clarinda’s bedside a wee tear came to her eyes. Poor Clarinda she thought, but she managed to hold back her feelings as she approached her Mum. But Maggie saw the sadness in Megan’s eyes. As they walked down the corridor Maggie says.
“Don’t worry Megan, Clarinda will be fine, and she’ll be home soon.”
Megan turned and looked up at her Mum, the tears started to run down her cheeks. Maggie started to cuddle Megan.
“It’s alright Megan, there’s nothing wrong with a good cry.”

As they were passing through the village of Torrance, Jock said.
“Who wants a fish supper?”
“Me.” Said Jamie, who was always hungry. “A could eat a wudden dumplin’ ahm starvin’.”
They all laughed at Jamie’s statement.
“Me too.” Said Megan.
“Can we get pickled onions Pappa?” Said Jamie.
“Aye, nae bother son.”
Jock and the kids got out at his house and Maggie went to Billie Rottenchips the local fish and chip shop to get the fish suppers.

And so a wee while later they were all sitting round a big roaring fire eating their fish suppers. Luath sat so proud looking from one to the other hoping for a chip. Luath was staring at Jamie with sad eyes, and he would cock his head from side to side, as if to say, “och don’t be rotten.” Jamie threw Luath a chip, Luath grabbed the chip in his mouth and suddenly threw the chip upwards, and the chip flew into the air and landed on Maggie’s head. Everybody burst out laughing; the laughter went on for quite some time.

“Did Luath mean that Pappa?” Said Jamie.
“No, the chip must have been too warm, or he did not like the vinegar. Anyway, please don’t do that again, but I must admit, it’s the best laugh I’ve had for a long time.”

"But Pappa, see the way Luath was looking at me with his sad eyes, a couldn'y help it." Said Jamie.
"Aye son I know, I think there's a wee bit of the fox in Luath, and he's a good actor too, so don't do it again, he's got those big black sad eyes joost like Rabbie Burns. Right let's get the dishes done, then we'll take Luath for a walk down to the Redwood Tree, and say a wee prayer for Clarinda."
"Yes." Shouted Jamie.
"I'll do the dishes Dad, away you go your walk, I'll see you round at my house." Said Maggie.
"Thanks Maggie, see you later."

A wee while later as they stood by the big Redwood Tree they each said a silent prayer for Clarinda. Jock said.
"The power of prayer is very important you know. You should never worry about anything. Every chance you get you should tell God about the things you want to ask him for. Especially in your prayers and your requests to him, and bring him your thanks as well. And God's peace, which is beyond our understanding and our contriving, will stand guard over our hearts and minds. Because your life is linked forever with the life of Jesus Christ."
Just then there was a flash of lighting right along the top of the Campsies.
"Did you see that Pappa?" Said Megan.
"Aye c'mon kids let's get home before we get soaked."
"C'mon Luath, let's go." Said Jamie.
"Aye, it's unusual to get thunder and lightning at this time of year, the weather is crazy nowadays. Hurry up kids."

After Jock had taken Megan and Jamie home he was passing the big house with Luath, and little did he know that he was being watched. Sheltering under the eaves just above Clarinda's bedroom window sat Robin Redbreast. He sat there patiently waiting and watching. For Robin Redbreast knew that Clarinda would be home soon. And he would be Clarinda's friend, that's why he was there.

After Jock had dried off Luath and changed out of his wet clothes, he sat by the inglenook (fireplace), and pondered on the day's events, he said to Luath.
"Aye, anither guid wee day Luath, Clarinda will be oot the hospital in a couple o' days and we'll have some smashing walks the gither. Aye and what aboot you Luath, throwing the chip on tae Maggie's head, yir no' real boy, come here tae a see you."
Luath jumped up on to Jock's lap and Jock gave him a wee cuddle.
"Aye, yir a bonnie dog right enough Luath."

Chapter 6

The Crambo Clinkers

It wasn't until the following Saturday that Clarinda was fit enough to go for a walk. She had got her 'Dallas' machine into the house and it made her feel better. And so off they went down on to the auld railway line for a wee daunder (walk). As they neared the spot where the Redwood Tree was, Megan said.
"Look Clarinda, there its there, the Redwood Tree."
"Wow, look at the size of it, it's beautiful."

They ran down the wee path to the water side, where stood the giant Sequoia. Megan said.
"You will have to give the Redwood a wee cuddle Clarinda."
"Why?" Asked Clarinda.
"Because it is a mystical tree, and will bring you luck and happiness and good health."
And so Clarinda and Jock and the kids all gave the tree a hug. Jamie says.
"Pappa, dae ye think the Redwood Tree knows we are giving it a wee cuddle?"
"Of course it does Jamie, it's living just like us, it will have feelings in a way that we do not understand, and maybe that's the way it should stay. I think that sometimes Man tries too find out too much about everything in this world, but then again why did God give us all brains, if not to think, well kids would you like to go up round Lennox Castle?"
"Is it safe Pappa, there's a lot of patients walking about up there?" Said Megan.
"Of course it's safe, some of the patients up there are wiser than some of the people outside, c'mon let's go."

"Pappa I have brought my poem with me that I wrote for the school competition." Said Megan.
"Oh good Megan, what's it called?"
'Happiness.' Said Megan.
"Well wait till we are up at the Castle and you can read it out to us. Wait till you see the snowdrops just in front of the Castle, and there's also another big Redwood there as well."
"Oh great, I love snowdrops, they are so gallant." Said Clarinda
What a strange thing for an eight-year-old girl to say, thought Jock.

They had just turned round the last bend at the top of the hill. And there stood the deserted Lennox Castle, what a waste thought Jock. Just over to the left stood the

huge Redwood, Jock told the kids to close their eyes, and then he slowly walked them over to the Redwood. Jock says.
"Right, open your eyes."
"Wow, fantastic." Said Clarinda.
"Oh look at that Pappa." Said Jamie.
"What a sight, is that not beautiful?" Said Jock.
Jock walked over and picked a single snowdrop.
"Come here kids and see one of the most beautiful sights that God has put on this earth."
He gently opened the snowdrop and showed the kids the inside of the flower; it was green, white and gold, absolutely gorgeous.
"That is amazing Pappa, can we take some home for Mum." Said Jamie.

They all collected a few flowers and put them into plastic bags. Then Jock took out a big flask from his haversack. He produced four plastic cups and poured the home-made soup. They all sat at the bottom of the Redwood Tree and sipped the hot broth. Jamie said.
"This is magic Pappa, any bread for the soup?"
"Och greedy guts Jamie." Said Megan.
"You'll get some sandwiches in a minute kids, just enjoy the view, okay Megan let's hear your poem."
Megan took out a piece of paper and began to read.

Happiness

By

Megan Mackenzie

Happiness is health not wealth,

Happiness is good not bad,

Happiness is love not hate,

Happiness is strong not weak,

Happiness is warm not cold,

Happiness is young and old,

Happiness cannot be bought nor sold.

"That is absolutely brilliant Megan." Said Jock. "I'm sure that's good enough to win any poetry competition, well done."

“That was lovely Megan, even Luath was listening when you were reading.” Said Clarinda.
“Oh thanks Clarinda.” Said Megan.

As they were walking down the back road from the castle, Jock said.
“Look over there kids, do you see that car going up the Crow Road?”
“Yes Papa, where does that road go?” Asked Megan.
“That’s the road to Fintry, and if you look just above you will see a line running at the same angle. That’s the old drover’s road. Before the Craw Road was there, that was the road the drover’s used to go over the Campsie Fells to Stirling market.”
“What’s a drover Pappa?” Asked Jamie.
“A drover is somebody who drives cattle and looks after them. We’ll go for a walk up there sometime, once the weather gets better, and I’ll tell you all about Rob Roy MacGregor a very famous Scotsman, and Benny Lynch, a world champion boxer who used to train in the Campsie Glen, and the Campsie Glen hotel where all the famous stars used to stay.”

“Did the Spice Girls stay there Pappa?” Asked Jamie.
“Och don’t be daft Jamie, see you, did the Spice Girls stay there! The Schoenstatt nuns have a retreat there now, the hotel was burned down, wasn’t it Pappa?”
“Thats right Megan, but anyway let’s go, when we get home I want to play you a song, it’s called ‘Redwood Tree’ by Van Morrison, you’ll love it.”

As they entered Jock’s house they could smell a wonderful aroma.
“Oh what’s that smell Pappa?” Said Jamie.
“That’s home made steak pie, and it’s just ready to eat, so get yir jaikets and shoes aff and yir Frankie Vaughn’s washed and set the table, I’ll serve it.”
So they all sat down and tucked in to the steak pie. Luath sat patiently waiting.
“This is brill Pappa.” Said Jamie. “A lot better than MacDonald’s.”
“Aye yir right enough there Jamie.” Said Jock.
Megan laughed and said.
“Aye, it’s the first time Jamie’s been quiet awe day.” They all laughed.
“Yes it’s lovely Jock thank you.” Said Clarinda.

After they had washed and dried all the dishes they all went into the living room. Jock went over to the music centre and put the Van Morrison CD on.
“Right kids here goes, now pay attention and listen to the words.”
They all sat back on the couch, Luath was sitting on Clarinda’s lap; he seemed to be very fond of Clarinda.

Redwood Tree.

Boy and the dog,
Went out looking for the rainbow,

And oh what did they learn,
Since they did that together.

Walking by the river,
And running like a blue streak,
Through the fields, streams and meadows,
Laughing all the way.

Oh Redwood Tree,
Please let us under,
When we were young we used to go,
Under the Redwood Tree.

And it smells like rain,
Maybe even thunder,
Won't you keep us from all harm?
Wonderful Redwood Tree.

Then the boy and his father,
Went out looking for the lost dog,
And oh what have they learned,
Since they did that together.

They did not bring him back,
He already had parted,
But look at everything they have learned,
Since that, since that very day.

And it smells like rain,
Maybe even thunder,
Won't you keep us from all harm?
Wonderful Redwood Tree.

"Oh that was great Pappa, gonny play it again please." Said Megan.
"Oh please Jock." Said Clarinda.
So Jock played the Redwood Tree half a dozen times, and soon they all knew it's every word, they loved it!
"Right kids that's the last time, get your shoes and jackets on, it's home time."

They walked round to the big house where Clarinda lived. She opened the big door and shouted.
"I'm home Mum." Her mother walked into the hallway and gave Clarinda a big cuddle.

"Did you have a good time?"
"It was fantastic Mum, look I got you some snowdrops."
"Thanks very much Jock for taking Clarinda with you."

"It's nae bother Janie, anytime, Clarinda's great company." Said Jock.
So they all said their cheerio's, and Jock took Megan and Jamie home.

About twenty minutes later Jock and Luath were passing the big house on their way home. Mr Brady came out to meet Jock. He said.
"Thanks very much Jock for taking Clarinda with you, she is so happy, it's really good for her."
"Whenever she's fit enough to go John we'll take her, it's a pleasure, she's a lovely wee lassie."
"Thanks Jock, do you fancy a pint tonight in the Auld Hoose?"
"That's joost aboot the best thing I've heard all day."
"See you tonight then Jock."
"Cheers John, see you later."

As Jock walked away, Robin Redbreast was sitting in the holly tree watching and listening. For Robin Redbreast was always watching, that's why he was there. And he soon would be introducing himself to Clarinda.

Chapter 7

The Man in the Moon

Later on that same evening in Auld Campsie Toun, the wind and the rain were having a rare ol' time. As Jock turned the key and left his house, he thought, thank God the Auld Hoose is just across the road. As he entered he saw auld Duncan sitting in his usual position, over by the corner in the lounge next to a roaring fire. He noticed that Duncan's glass was full and he was in the company of a stranger.

"Hi Jock, what a night eh!" Said Duncan.
"Terrible Duncan, you're no' daft eh, you've got the best seat in the house."
"Well Jock, when you get to my age you can have this seat, anyway dae ye ken this man here?"
"I know the face but I joost canny place it."
"This is my son Douglas." Said Duncan.
Jock and Douglas shook hands.
"Pleased to meet you Douglas, I remember you now, but it's been years."
"How do you do Jock, I remember you, but it's been a while since I've been back in Campsie." Said Douglas.
"Aye, they always come back tae Campsie, every one of them. No matter who it is, no matter where they go, they always come hame. It's like a magnet, your home that is, somehow you must go back, it's inherent, it's in your genes. It's just like the salmon used to be in the Glazert river, one day they will return, there is no doubt about it, you mark my words." Said auld Duncan.
"Aye, I quite agree with you there Duncan." Said Jock.
"And talking about salmon Jock, Douglas has brought me a couple if nice ones down from Callander, I'll give you some for Maggie and the weans, especially that Jamie, what an appetite that boy has got."
"Great Duncan, thanks, I hope it's not poached salmon Douglas." Said Jock with a wry smile.
"Oh no Jock, you'll have to cook it yourself." Said Douglas with an even wryer smile.
"Aye he's definitely your son Duncan, there's nae doubt about that." Said Jock as he lifted his pint of beer.
"Cheers." Said Douglas.
"Aye cheers Sergeant Douglas MacGregor." Said Duncan.
Jock nearly choked on his pint.
"Whit? Sergeant, in the Polis'?"

“Aye, Douglas is a Sergeant awa’ up near Callander.”
“Well, ‘I’ll enjoy the salmon all the more, cheers.” Said Jock

About twenty minutes later Clarinda’s Dad John and Thomas ‘Bamber’ McLaughlin joined the company. Thomas like auld Duncan had a great memory and could remember all the old stories and the old characters of Campsie.
As the landlord Willie Boyle put more logs and coal on the fire. Thomas said.
“Talking about salmon, I heard a wee fishy story the other day.”
Everybody listened as “Bamber” told the story.

“This Scottish guy went down to Manchester to start work on the building of a new supermarket. His name was John, okay? So he arrives at the guesthouse on the Sunday night, and the landlady says to him.
“John do you like fish?”
Well it so happened that John loved fish.
“Oh yes I certainly do Mrs Jones.”
“That’s good, I’m getting some lovely kippers delivered in the morning, and you can have some for breakfast.”
“Oh great.” Said John.
So the following morning John had his kippers, and thought, this is magic, the best guesthouse I’ve ever been in. As he finished his breakfast the landlady says to him.
“Did you enjoy that John?”
“Fantastic Mrs Jones.”
“Oh call me Val, please. Well John, I know your job is only two minutes walk from here, I’m getting some nice cod delivered for lunch, would you like that?”
“Oh that would be nice Val.” Said John, in his best Kelvinside accent.
“Okay John, see you at lunch.”
So lunchtime came and John had his cod, and Val said
“Did you enjoy that John?”
“Oh Val, that was absolutely brilliant.”
“Just you wait till tonight, I’ve got something special for your dinner.”
John couldn’y wait.
That night it was Dover sole for dinner, and then the following morning it was kippers again. All week it went on fish, fish, fish! John thought there was something fishy going on. And then on the Friday night John went for a few beers with the lads on the building site. But the beer led to whisky and the whisky led to a sore heid in the morning. And John was working on Saturday morning.”
Thomas took a swig of his beer and went on.

“So the following morning John took his seat at the dining table, his head was thumping. He could smell the fish from the kitchen, he started to boak, oh no. The landlady walked up to John’s table, and as she put the kippers down she accidentally knocked over the salt.”

“Oh my God.” She said. “That must be an omen or luck, or maybe a strange man is coming to the house today.” John answered quickly.
“I hope tae God it’s the butcher.”
Everybody laughed.
“Aye very good Thomas.” Said Duncan.

So then the jokes and the stories started to fly. Then Jock said.
“Did yous hear the wan about God and Jesus and the Pope when they were playing a game of golf?”
“No.” Said John.
And so Jock proceeded to tell his tale.
“Well a massive congregation had gathered round the eighteenth green, there was thousands watching. God ‘Jimmy McDonald’ had been playing terrible, and he knew he had to play a miraculous shot to win the match. Jesus and the Pope were playing well and were all-square.

The Pope stepped up to the tee and placed his ball. He blessed the ball and then he blessed the crowd. He swung his seven iron and hit a brilliant shot just six inches from the hole. The crowd went wild, what a shot. ‘Jimmy McDonald’ was ragin’ mad.

Then Jesus steps up to the tee with his new dress on, wallop, the ball bounced on the green and rolled up three inches short of the hole. Fantastic, the crowd went crazy, what a match.
One spectator was heard to say. ‘If the Big Man disn’y win this hole we are all doomed.’
God was ragin’, he now needed an eagle to win the match. He placed his ball and swung his seven iron, the Pope farted, and ‘Jimmy Mac’ sliced his ball skywards. The Pope was shittin’ himself in case he lost his job. ‘Tae hell wi’ that Job Centre’ he thought.

Then all of a sudden a Golden Eagle swooped from the sky and caught God’s ball in its mouth, and carried it towards the green. God turned and smiled at Jesus and the Pope. As the crowd looked up to the sky the eagle dropped the ball into a bunker, the crowd sighed, Oh No, No. Just then a wee rabbit ran oot a hole in the ground and lifted ‘Jimmy Macs’ ball, and sprinted towards the green. The wee rabbit whose name was Shuggy, by the way, ran up to the hole and dropped Gods’ ball in. The crowd was absolutely stunned; it was a Miracle!
Then Jesus turned round and said to God.
“C’mon Da gees a brek Big Man, it’s only a game.”
Everybody laughed.
“Brilliant Jock.”

A wee while later Thomas told a story about an old butcher from Kirkintilloch.

"I'll tell yees a wee story aboot this butcher called Pender Broon. But first, I just remembered one of wee Rod's pals. His name was Charlie, Charlie had been a miner all his days and the poor guy had paid the price of working down the pits. His body was bent at a right angle. He used tae walk in to Carlin's pub, and this is true, he would be standing at the bar and his head was the same height as the bar. He would turn his head and shout.
'Gimme a hauf and a hauf pint Jimmuck. Has the Rod been in?'
'No yit.' Said Jimmuck.
Well he would stand there drinking his beer and whisky, havin' a blether wi' the locals. And the more he drank the straighter he would become. After about ten whiskies he would be standing up straight, honest tae God."
"Aye, the power o' John Barleycorn." Said auld Duncan.
"Whit aboot this Pender Broon , Thomas?" Asked Douglas.

"Away back in the early sixties I was standing in the Burns Tavern havin' a pint. I got talking to this auld guy and this is what happened."
"Whit's your name son?"
"McLaughlin." Said Thomas.
"Are ye local?"
"Aye."
"Whose yir faither?"
"Pat McLaughlin."
"Och I know him well, do you know who I am son?"
"Sorry I don't, who are you?"
"I'm Pender Broon, the famous butcher from Kirkintilloch."
"Och aye, ah've heard of you."
"I've got the best butcher meat in Scotland son, have ye no' tasted ma sausages?"
"Sorry I have not."
"Aye the best in the west. Huv ye no' seen the big sign ootside ma shop at Kirkie Cross? People come from all over joost tae get thir squares and links fae Pender Broon."
"What's on the sign Pender?"
"The sign says."

IF PENDER BROON
WAS THE MAN IN THE MOON
WHIT WOULD YEES DAE FUR YIR SAUSAGES?

"That's a cracker Thomas." Said Jock
"Aye, what a man, Pender Broon wis."

A wee while later as Jock was walking home with Mr Brady, he said.
“John, see today when the kids and I were away up at Lennox Castle, and we came across the snowdrops, and I showed them the inside of one.”
“Aye, what about it Jock?”
“When Clarinda saw it, she said, ‘very gallant’, I wonder what she meant?”
“I don’t know Jock, Clarinda is very intelligent you know. Anyway, I must go, I really enjoyed the company tonight Jock, must do it again sometime.”
“Aye surely John, goodnight.”

Chapter 8

The Carron Dam Walk

As Clarinda was released from the velvet dreams of the Sandman, she heard a noise at her bedroom window. She looked over towards the window but could see nothing. The bottom panes of the window were covered in condensation. The noise went on bick, bick, bick, so she got up and went over and wiped the window. And there he was fluttering up and down, Robin Redbreast wanted to say hello. She smiled, and quickly opened the window. Robin Redbreast flew over to the holly tree and then dived down to the garden table.

Clarinda quickly got dressed and ran down the stairs shouting to her Mum and Dad and telling them what had happened. Clarinda got some bread and cornflakes and went outside and threw them over to Robin Redbreast. He started to eat right away.
"That's you got a new friend Clarinda." Said her Mum.
"It's very strange Mum, he more or less asked me to feed him; why did he come and knock on my window?"
"Well maybe he knows that you are a nice person and that you would give him something to eat."
"It's very strange Mum."

Just at that moment Jamie and Megan were passing with Luath. Clarinda shouted to them to come into the garden. She told them all about the wee robin knocking on the window. Megan said.
"Maybe you will be able to train him to eat from your hand Clarinda."
"Oh yes Megan, but that would take time."
"Right Clarinda." Said her Mum. "It's a wee bit cold out here, and Jamie and Megan are going to be late for school, say bye bye."
"See you later Clarinda when we get home from school." Said Jamie.
"Bye." Said Megan, who always felt a wee bit of sadness every time she left Clarinda.
"Remember and come back to see me." Said Clarinda.
Megan could see in Clarinda's eyes that she was wishing that she was going a walk and then going to school, but she would have to take it easy.

As Jamie and Megan reached Jock's house he was waiting for them with their school bags.

"C'mon kids, get a move on or we are gonny be late for school, we'll have a quick walk down the railway and then cut up to the school."
When they reached the bottom of the school lane Megan asked her Pappa where he was going with Luath.
"We're going up the Crow Road, but don't worry I'll take you up there very soon, now awa' up tae the school and get educated, awa' yees go."
Before they went Jock gave Megan and Jamie a wee cuddle, and off they went. Jock learned many years ago from his old grandmother that you should always say something nice to loved ones every time you leave them, or give them a wee cuddle, for it may be the last time you see them.

As Jock walked up the Crow Road past the Campsie golf course, he looked down at Luath and said.
"Aye Luath, Spring is in the air boy, can you not smell it?" the daffodils and crocuses will soon be blooming, and smell that fresh air Luath this is the life, the open road, the hills and peace of mind, aye the greatest things in life boy. It disnae cost any money to do this Luath, no, not a penny."

As they turned past the big house on the hill Jock and Luath went over to an old spring called McKinney's Well.
"C'mon Luath and get a drink of this lovely water."
Jock cupped his hands and took a drink; the water was ice cold. When he had finished drinking he then gave Luath some water. Jock remembered the stories his father used to tell him years ago about how the local men used to come up to McKinney's Well every Sunday to drink the beautiful water. Some said that the water had iron and minerals in it and was really good for you. Another reason they drank from the spring was that they were all skint, and if they had the money they would have been in the pub. But in those days the pubs did not open on a Sunday and the wages they got from working down pits and working in foundries was a disgrace to human society. But the men loved the spring water and the walks up the Campsies.
Jock remembered something his father always used to say.
"I'd rather be up the top of the Meikle Bin than doon a bloody pit."

As Jock and Luath reached the top of the Crow Road they sat down on the seat overlooking the 'Crooked Valley.' The view was tremendous, he could see away over to the Dumbarton Hills in the southwest, and if he looked away over to the southeast he could see the Lead Hills, and that's where the source of the River Clyde started. And so there was Jock sitting on his favourite seat with his wee pal Luath. Jock took out his pipe, while Luath tried to watch every sheep down in the valley. And then all of a sudden it hit Jock. The past! Mary!

He started to reminisce about his wife who had died ten years ago. There were times when she would be completely out of his mind, then bang, she would come back to his thoughts like a bolt of lightning, especially when he was walking up the Crow Road, because that's where it all started; the first long walk Mary and him had had together, that was the day they fell in love, the day of the Carron Dam walk. And what a walk that turned out to be, they were so wrapped up in each other and talking of the future that the time and the miles flew by wi' tentless heed.
"Ten years Luath, aye ten years, where did it go, ach Mary I miss you so much. Why, oh why, did God have to take her away from me, she was only forty eight?"

Luath was looking up at Jock; Jock turned his head and looked down into Luath's eyes. Two small tears ran down Jock's face, and then Luath moved up slowly and licked his master's tears. It was obvious that Luath knew Jock was very sad. Jock lifted Luath and started to cuddle him.
"Aye she would have loved you Luath, just as she loved me, and me her. Thank God I've still got Maggie, she's her Mammies double. And Megan and Jamie, they didn'y even know her, they've only seen her on a daft video."
But Jock knew that he had to remember the good times. Then he started to reflect on the day his 'Highland Mary,' as he called her, walked all the way round the Carron Dam.

He could never forget that beautiful sunny Sunday morning. He met Mary outside the Town Hall and off they went up the Crow Road. As they got to the top of the Campsie Glen they sat down to eat some fruit, and as they looked down to the bottom of the Glen they could see hundreds of people walking about. Some were sat down with their picnics, while others were paddling in the Kirk Burn. And the brave ones would be swimming in the ice cool Linns.

They came from all over to the Campsie Glen in those days, from all parts of Glasgow and the West of Scotland, but Jock and Mary were more interested in each other than anything else. And so they tramped on past Jimmy Wright's Well, and onwards on the road to Fintry. As they strolled along on that glorious day, each would steal a glance at the other, then their eyes would meet and they would smile. Every time Jock looked into Mary's eyes, he would get a tingling sensation all over, and Mary felt exactly the same. They both seemed to know that this was the real thing, even though they had only met two weeks ago.

Half an hour later they passed Jimmy McKeowns' Half Way House, then about a mile along the road they decided to have their own wee picnic, away from the eyes of the world. After they had eaten they lay back and soaked in the sun. Mary moved closer to Jock and lay in the crook of his left arm. A wee while later Jock looked down at Mary and she was fast asleep. Jock was smiling to himself, he was so happy, for this was surely the loveliest day of his life, he wished it could last for ever and ever.

Then he suddenly remembered the poem he had brought to show Mary, it was 'Sweet Afton' by Robert Burns.

He gently took the poem from his waistcoat and started to read.

Flow gently, sweet Afton, among thy green braes!
Flow gently, I'll sing thee a song in thy praise!
My Mary's asleep by thy murmuring stream-
Flow gently, sweet Afton, disturb not her dream!

Thou stock dove whose echo resounds thro' the glen,
Ye wild whistling Blackirds in yon thorny den
Thou green-crested lapwing, thy screaming forbear-
I charge you, disturb not my slumbering fair.

How lofty, sweet Afton, thy neighbouring hills,
Far mark'd with the courses of clear, winding rills!
There daily I wander, as noon rises high,
My flocks, and my Mary's sweet cot in my eye.

How pleasant thy banks and green vallies below,
Where wild in the woodlands the primroses blow'
There oft' as mild evenin' weeps over the lea,
The sweet-scented birk shades my Mary and me.

Thy crystal stream, Afton, how lovely it glides,
And winds by the cot where my Mary resides,
How wanton thy waters her snowy feet lave,
As, gathering sweet flowerets, she stems thy clear wave!

Flow gently, sweet Afton, among thy green braes,
Flow gently, sweet river, the theme of my lays!
My Mary's asleep by thy murmuring stream,
Flow gently, sweet Afton, disturb not her dream!

It was about five minutes later that Mary awoke, and she said.
"Oh Jock I'm sorry, I didn't realise how tired I was."
"That's alright Mary, it must have been the sun, but anyway I was enjoying looking at you as I was reading this poem. C'mon down to the burn and I will present it to you."

They walked down to the burn and Jock jumped across to the other side. He knelt down and offered the poem up to Mary as he said.

"Mary I've been wanting to say this to you since the day I met you."
"What is it Jock?"
"Mary I love you, you are so beautiful, I want you to be my wife."
"Oh Jock I love you too, and I will be your wife."
Jock felt fantastic, as did Mary; he jumped across the burn and slipped on a wet stone and fell into the arms of Mary. They both fell to the ground laughing their heads off, and then they kissed.

A wee while later they got back on the road and headed down the hill in to Fintry. The view away over to the west was fantastic; you could just see Loch Lomond at the foot of Ben Lomond.
"Look at that Mary, is that not something?"
"It's absolutely breathtaking Jock."
"Aye, it must be one of the best views in Scotland."

And so they walked on till they reached the Carron Dam. Half an hour later they went into the Carronbridge and had a pint of shandy each. And then on they went down the Tak' Ma Doon Road into Kilsyth. They had made a thousand plans and talked endlessly about the future. In no time at all they were walking past the Tar-Row, at the entrance to Auld Campsie Toun.

Jock finally snapped out of his reverie, and said to Luath.
"Ach memories Luath, whit wud we dae withoot them. Let's go boy, ah've got a pot of soup tae make fur the dinner, we'll go and get Jamie and Megan after school."

Later on that night as Jock sat by the fire, he said to Luath.
"Aye, it's been a good day Luath. Did you enjoy that wee walk the day, aye, and the ham oot the soup?"
Luath who was stretched out by the fire, just looked up at Jock and winked.
"Aye, you're no daft Luath, eh!"

Chapter 9

Dunblame

That morning was just like any other morning for Jock and the kids. They would take Luath down along the auld railway line and on to the Field Park and teach him how to sit and walk properly with and without the lead. Luath was a quick learner and it would not be long till Jock had him house-trained, and the kids would be able to take him to stay at their house. But little did they know at that time what was about to happen in Scotland.

Neither did anybody else, except a man named Thomas Hamilton, who, that morning, would commit one of the most terrible and horrific crimes ever committed in Scottish history. Murder is bad enough, but when it's innocent children and an innocent teacher. It's impossible to comprehend.

Jock left the kids at the bottom of the school road and went for a walk up the auld railway line. He walked on about halfway up to Strathblane just across from Ballagan falls. He sat down on an old railway sleeper and had his sandwiches and a wee drink along with Luath. Ten minutes later they started back home. It must have been about lunchtime when Jock and Luath arrived back in Auld Campsie Toun. As Jock walked down the main street he met an old friend of his called Ernie.

"Hi Jock, how you doin?" Said Ernie.
"Not bad Ernie how's yirsel?"
"Not bad Jock, did you hear the terrible news on the radio?"
"Naw, whit's happened noo?"
"Well it seems some madman went berserk up in a school in Dunblane and shot about a dozen children, there's still reports coming in." Said Ernie.
"Oh my God, surely not Ernie, that canny be true."
"Honest Jock, it's the truth."

Jock hurried on down to the house and quickly turned on the telly, and sure enough it was true. Jock sat down and listened in disbelief. He was stunned. "Oh Jesus Christ almighty have mercy on them, the poor wee souls, what kind of a monster could do that?" Jock said to himself and Luath.

Later on it was reported that sixteen children and one teacher had been shot in cold blood. The murderer was a man named Thomas Hamilton. After he shot the innocents, the cowardly bastard shot himself. The tears welled up in Jock's eyes; he couldn't help but cry. Two minutes later he phoned Maggie.

“I canny believe it Dad, it’s a nightmare, they poor weans.”
“The terrible thing about it is, is that it could happen anywhere Maggie, I’ll go up to the school with you at three o’clock.”

“Oh my God, what about Jamie and Megan, and all the other kids, how are they gonny feel Dad?” Maggie started to cry.
‘I’ll be there in five minutes’. Said Jock.

Two minutes later as Jock passed the big house where Clarinda lived, he could see her feeding the wee robin. He stood and watched her for a few moments and thought, ‘God, how on earth do you tell a wee girl like Clarinda what’s just happened, how do you explain it, what can you say?’ He didn’t bother to say hello, somehow he just couldn’t.

But the sad fact remained, the children had to be told, because it had happened to children and it had happened in a school, which made it all the more harrowing. Tragedies happened every other day, but none like Dunblane. They say that time is a great healer, well there must be doubts about that statement. Jock walked into Maggie’s house, she was sitting watching the telly. She was holding a towel and her eyes were all bloodshot. She says.
“It’s sixteen children and one teacher now Dad, how could that happen? For God’s sake, they’re only wee babies.”

Jock went over and gave Maggie a wee cuddle as she started to cry again. ‘How indeed did God let these things happen,’ thought Jock.
“Ach, is it not a terrible world we live in Maggie, the kids are gonny take this very hard, how can they understand what’s happened.”
“I know Dad, it’s awful, look at Luath, the way he is looking at us.”
Luath was cocking his head from one side to the other with a sad look in his eyes. Maggie started to laugh and cry at the same time.
“Well at least he makes you laugh Maggie.” Said Jock.
Maggie lifted Luath up and gave him a wee cuddle, and said.
“Aye, yir a bonny wee dog Luath.”

Later on that afternoon when the kids were home they asked Maggie and Jock how anybody could do such a terrible thing. Jock and Maggie were both stumped for answers. All Jock could say was.
“Well kids, there are a lot of good people in the world, but sadly there are a few bad ones. How God could let that happen? Well, I canny answer that, I don’t think anybody could. One thing for sure is, they will all be in Heaven, and we must never forget them, so remember them in your prayers tonight.”
“We will Pappa, we will.” Said Jamie and Megan.

Before Jock left he promised the kids that after Mass on Sunday, which was St Patrick's day, he would take them to a secret place where they would get loads of daffodils and they would all go up to Dunblane with them. Jamie said.
"Can we take Clarinda with us Pappa?"

"Aye, certainly Jamie, we sure can."
"Whit about Luath, will he be able to go Pappa?" Said Megan.
"Of course he can go, and we'll get fish suppers on the way back, because it's Maggie's turn to pay."
"Oh great Pappa, that Luath just loves fish and chips." Said Jamie.

That night as Jock sat in front of a roaring fire drinking his penny-wheep, he said to Luath.
"Ach't it's been a bad day the day Luath, what a weird world we live in son, eh, it's alright for you, you're joost a wee dog with no' a care in the world."
Luath just lifted his head off the fireside rug and looked at Jock. He winked at Jock and then went back to Noddyland.

The following Sunday after Mass at St Machan's, Maggie and Jock and the kids went to the secret place where the daffodils were. As they walked through the woods Jock told them to be as quiet as possible. They heard a tapping noise and Megan asked Jock what it was.
"That was a spotted woodpecker, listen, did you hear it again?" Said Jock.
"Aye." They all said quietly.
"Shoosh, did you hear another one over there?"
"Aye."
"That's its mate sending a message with its beak on the tree."
"That's amazing Pappa." Said Jamie.
"Isn't it? That's what they call tree-mail." Said Jock.
They all burst out laughing. Jock said.
"Look Megan, all the snowdrops have gone back to sleep till next year, but wait till you see the daffodils."

They came to a clearing and beheld a wondrous site. There were thousands of flowers scattered all over the clearing; the kids and Maggie could not believe their eyes.
"I've never seen so many daffodils." Said Clarinda. "It's so beautiful here."
"Look Mum." Said Megan.
"It's lovely." Said Maggie.
"Right kids, let us pick a few bunches." Said Jock.
And so they each picked a couple of bunches. There were orange ones, white ones, red ones, all different kinds, then off they went to Dunblane.

To say it was a sad experience would be an understatement, but Jock thought that going to Dunblane would somehow help the children to understand. Maybe it was the wrong thing to do he thought, but at least they would be making a statement that they cared, and cared deeply by delivering the daffodils, and that was about all anybody could do, was care.

On the way back home the kids went a bit quiet, which was understandable, after what they had done. Jock says.
"Who disny want a fish supper?"
Silence.
"Everybody wants a fish supper." Said Maggie. "Even Luath."

Later on after everybody had gone home, Jock thought about going for a beer to the Auld Hoose, but changed his mind and settled for an early night and a good book. He said to Luath.
"Aye Luath, peace of mind and guid health ye canny whack it, and a wee bit of peace and quiet, the best things in the world. Would you look at you, lickin' yir lips, a' think there's a wee bit o' the cat in you, the way you ate that fish, aye and a wee bit o' the fox as well!"
Luath just gave Jock a look of complete innocence.

Dunblame

Seventeen spirits dancing on the brook,
I can hear them laughing,
Whilst, telling them tales,
Of snowdrops and daffodils,
And yellow wagtails.

One bad apple, that stopped all the games,
That stopped all the play,
Why must these things happen?
I hear you say.

There's a terrible madness,
In this world of ours,
And we must live with it,
Until it devours.

But cheer up, there's five billion people,
With hope and many good tales,
Who love the snowdrops, and daffodils,
And yellow wagtails.

Chapter 10

Murder in Campsie

The month of March came and went as quickly as January and February. And now it was the turn of April to spread its showers down on Auld Campsie Toun. Luath was spending two and three nights a week at Jamie and Megan's house, now that he was house trained. But every morning they would always go to their Pappa's and leave Luath there before going to school. But most morning's their Pappa would walk up to school with them.

And every morning they would call in on Clarinda to see how she was and ask her to go for a walk. But most mornings she could not go because she felt tired. She would always say.
"Hopefully I'll be alright tomorrow."
And then she would whistle and Robin Redbreast would appear and she would smile as she threw him something to eat. It would not be long till she would be able to hand feed him.

Then before going to school, Jamie and Megan and Jock would walk down to the Redwood Tree with Luath and they would always say a silent prayer for Clarinda. Then after school they went for another wee daunder and then home for dinner.
After dinner Jock said to Maggie.
"Well Maggie I think I'll go for a pint tonight, there's usually a wee song-song in the Auld Hoose."
"Right Dad, have a nice night, see you tomorrow."

Half an hour later Jock was sitting alongside auld Duncan, his drouthie cronie. The fire was blazing in the wee lounge, while the potential singers were lubricating their vocal chords at the bar. As the pub began to fill up a couple of guys came in, one with a guitar and the other with a violin. Jock mentioned Dunblane to Duncan, and they talked about it for a wee while, but they felt so helpless. Then suddenly three pints of beer appeared along with Thomas as he sat down next to Jock and Duncan.
"Cheers Thomas." Said Duncan.
"Awe the best." Said Jock.
"Well boys, did you ever hear the story about the murder in Campsie, away back in the seventeenth century?" Asked Duncan.
"Have not." Said Thomas.

“Away back then a new minister came to Campsie; his name was John Collins and he was a confirmed bachelor, but that was about to change. He fell in love and married one of the loveliest and most sought after women in the district, and there were many disappointed suitors who gave up when she married Mr Collins, except one, the Laird of Balglass. The Laird had pursued the lady, but to no avail, and so he decided that the minister would have to leave the Planet.”

“Aye very good Duncan, I like it.” Said Thomas. Duncan went on.
“The Laird became friendly with the minister, and was a regular guest at the Manse, but little did the minister or his wife know what was on the Laird’s mind. Jealously and hatred were building up inside the Laird, but he could conceal it at first. Eventually, when he could conceal it no longer, a dastardly plan was hatched.

It was one night in November 1648 when the Laird knew that the minister would be in Glasgow for a Presbytery meeting, that he decided he would send the minister to meet his maker, in other words, *murder him.* Balglass went along the Glasgow road and waited at a dark part of the route. The minister arrived on horseback, and Balglass dragged him from his horse and murdered him. He took his victim’s watch and money so that suspicion might fall on highwaymen. He left the body by the roadside and made for home.

The minister’s horse arrived back at the Manse without its owner. Mrs Collins, anxious about her husband’s safety, ran to her neighbours, and a search party was organised. A messenger ran to Balglass for help. The Laird had anticipated this, and he hastened to the manse. He joined in the search, and even helped to carry the body home. He then broke the news to Mrs Collins, who collapsed.”
“A very devious man, this Balglass eh, all because of jealously!” Said Jock.
“Go on Duncan, what happened next?” Said Thomas.

“Well Balglass gave Mrs Collins more and more attention, and said he would find the murderer. He said nothing about marriage until it became necessary for Mrs Collins to leave the Manse, to make way for her husband’s successor. At first she refused to listen to his proposal, but, having no home to go to she gave way, and they were married. His villainy had triumphed.

He was happy for a time, and then his conscience started to trouble him. He could not sleep, he became restless, evaded company and refused to talk. His conduct made his wife anxious, so she resolved to seek the cause of his trouble. She thought that some light might be thrown on the mystery, if she could examine his papers, which were kept in a box. He guarded the key jealously, but eventually she secured it. So one day she opened the box and examined the contents. And in the corner she found her dead husband’s watch. Suddenly Balglass appeared.

She looked up and saw the guilt written on her husband's face, and realised that she had sacrificed herself to her husband's murderer, then she fainted."
"Did he get caught Duncan?"Asked Jock.
"No, apparently he fled the country, and she died. Murder in Campsie eh!" "Are yees fur another beer lads?" Said Duncan.
"Certainly Duncan, cheers."

And then the singsong was about to start. A few jokes were told and then Jock told the guys all about the kids and how he called them the Crambo Clinkers, and how he encouraged them to read and write poetry.

"Here's a wee poem I wrote aboot a wee pal o' mine." Said Jock.

Big Ann and the Wee Man

Big Ann went into the van,
Looking fur the wee man,
The wee man wus doon in the pub,
Drinking a black n' tan.

Whit's his game! Thought Big Ann,
As she lay on the big black divan,
I'll sort him oot,
That dastardly wee man.

The wee man finished his tenth black n' tan,
And said, Cheerio boys,
I'm off tae see Big Ann
Up in the big black divan, in the van.

As the wee man sneaked in tae the van,
He got walloped on the heid wi' a can,
And that wus the end,
Of the wee man and Big Ann.

"Aye very good Jock, that was funny'." Said auld Duncan.

A wee while later the singsong was in full flow. John, Clarinda's father came back from the toilet and said that Tam McIvor was going to sing 'Ae Fond Kiss.' As Tam started to sing the whole pub went silent. John loved the song, as it was about Nancy McElhose one of Rabbies great loves. Burns called her 'Clarinda,' and that was how John's daughter Clarinda got her name.

Ae Fond Kiss

Ae fond kiss, and then we sever!
Ae farewell, and then forever!
Deep in heart wrung tears I'll pledge thee,
Warring sighs and groans I'll wage thee.

Who shall say that Fortune grieves him,
While the star of hope she leaves him?
Me, nae cheerfu' twinkle lights me,
Dark despair around benights me.

I'll ne'er blame my partial fancy:
Naething could resist my Nancy,
But to see her was to love her,
Love but her, and love for ever.

Had we never lov'd sae kindly'
Had we never lov'd sae blindly,
Never met-or never parted-
We had ne'er been broken-hearted.

Fare-thee-weel, thou first and fairest!
Fare-thee-weel, thou best and dearest!
Thine be ilka joy and treasure,
Peace, Enjoyment, Love and Pleasure!.

Ae fond kiss, and then we sever!
Ae farewell, alas, for ever!
Deep in heart-wrung tears I'll pledge thee,
Warring sighs and groans I'll wage thee.

There was thunderous applause for Tam as he finished.
"That was brilliant." Said auld Duncan.
"Aye, try following that!" Said Jock.

Chapter 11

The Three Steps

Never cast a cloot till May is oot. Well, May came and went and now June was in its glory. The sun was shining and the temperature was in the high seventies. Jock had promised the kids that once the weather got better that he would take them camping up the Campsies and camp out overnight.

The Three Steps are three cliffs that have formed at the front of the Campsies millions of years ago, when Auld Campsie Toun was covered in ice and then water. You can actually find seashells at the bottom of the Three Steps. Jock phoned Maggie and asked to speak to Megan and Jamie.
"Hi Megan, the weather is going to be great today, and a clear sky tonight, would you and Jamie like to go camping tonight up to the Three Steps?"
"Oh yes Pappa, that would be great, I'll phone Clarinda and see if she will be well enough to come with us." Said Megan.
"Right Megan, we'll set out at six o'clock tonight, and get the tent pitched by eight; see you tonight."

Maggie came back on the phone and said.
"What time will you be back in the morning Dad?"
"I don't know Maggie, it depends on the kids, and they've never done this before."
"I wouldn't worry about that Dad, they won't want to come back home."
"Aye you might be right enough there Maggie."

So later on Megan and Jamie and Luath, who was getting bigger every day and more wise, and could now wink with both eyes, set out on their first camping night. They were so excited as they said cheerio to their Mum.
"Remember and behave yourselves, and do what your Pappa tells you, remember and come back." Said Maggie.
"A umny comin' back Mam, ah'm gonny stay up the hills forever." Said Jamie.
"Ach don't listen to him Mam, he's aff his napper." Said Megan.
"Och awa' yees go, yous will probably be wanting home when it gets dark." Said Maggie.
"That'll be right, cheerio the noo Mammy." Said Jamie, laughing.

So off went the campers. They called in to Clarinda's house where Jock was already waiting for them. They walked up the Craw Road past the big house on the hill, then up to McKinney's Well, which was just behind the Campsie Golf Course at the bottom of the 'Three Steps.' They sat down at the well to have a drink, and

Jock told the kids all about its history. He told them that the water was really good to drink because of its natural minerals. Jamie took a drink and said.
"That watter's smashin' Pappa, Ah could drink it awe day."

"You're no' real Jamie, if you drink any more you wont be able to walk up to the Three Steps, will he Pappa?" Said Megan.
"Aye Megan's right Jamie, let's fill a couple of bottles and we'll get going." Said Jock.
"Where does that watter come from Pappa, it's always running?" Said Jamie.
"Aye your right there Jamie, I'll tell you all about runnin' water once we get the tent pitched, now lets get going."

They slowly made their way up to the Three Steps and found a nice wee flat area surrounded by rocks, where they pitched their tent. The view was brilliant.
"What a lovely view Pappa." Said Megan.
"It's absolutely glorious Jock." Said Clarinda.
"Look away over to the west kids, and just watch as the sun goes down." Said Jock.
"Where does the sun go Pappa?" Asked Jamie.
"It does not go anywhere, see the daft questions you ask." Said Megan.
"Well what happens is this. The earth is slowly turning and the sun appears to disappear, but the sun is moving as well, so in a way you are both right. But do you know what the sun is?" Said Jock.
"It's a star." Said Clarinda.
"That's right Clarinda, and so are you, well done." Said Jock.
"Och A knew that." Said Jamie.
"Aye so you did." Said Megan. "That'll be right!"
"Och stop arguing you two, we are here to enjoy ourselves and to learn things. Do you remember the running water down at McKinney's Well?" Said Jock.
"Yes Pappa." Said Megan.

"Okay, now picture this. Away back in 1768 when Robert Burns was only nine years old, just about ages with the three of you, he did not have many of the things in his house which you now take for granted. Said Jock."
"I know what you are going to say Jock." Said Clarinda.
"Good for you Clarinda, but can you just imagine it? First of all, running water from a tap in your house. Not just cold water, but hot water. Electric light when you press a switch, cookers, washing machines, fridges and hoovers. None of these things were invented when Robert Burns was a wee boy." Said Jock.

"Wus there any television Pappa?" Said Jamie.
"Och Jamie your nuts." Said Megan, laughing.
"No, nae televisions, nae videos, nae phones, nae play stations, no' even any Spice Girls either, they lived in dire poverty. Electricity never came to Campsie until the 1930's. And that's only sixty odd years ago."

"Not very long ago!" Said Clarinda.
"Indeed, so the next time you turn on a light switch or turn on a tap, just think how lucky you are."

As the sun was slowly sinking beyond the horizon the Crambo Clinkers were getting ready for the stars to appear. It was a beautiful night and Auld Campsie Toun lay silently down below in the Crooked Valley. The honest men and bonnie lasses would be quenching their thirsts in the local taverns, for it sure was a thirsty nicht the nicht.

The light was slowly disappearing and the stars would soon be coming out all over the night sky.
"Now kids, I want you to be totally quiet, do not say a thing. Just look and listen, listen to the sound of silence."
Jock took out the sandwiches and a big flask of tea from his rucksack and passed them round to the children.
"Now have your tea, and remember no talking."
Jamie couldn't help whispering into Clarinda's ear.
"This is magic Clarinda, isn't it?"
Clarinda just smiled at Jamie with her finger at her mouth.

A wee while later it was Megan who noticed the first star.
"Look Pappa, there's a star."
"Well done Megan, just wait about five minutes and you'll see hundreds." Said Jock.
Then Jamie and Clarinda spotted stars, they were appearing all over the night sky, and then Jamie said.
"See that Patrick Moore Pappa, A think he's dead funny."
Jock laughed and said.
"Well he doesn't mean to be funny, he's a very intelligent man."
Jock knew it was going to be a long night, for the kids were so excited it would be very difficult for them to sleep. He wondered what wee Jamie was going to ask next, he sure had a very inquisitive mind, and that was a good thing to see in any child.

"Whereabouts up there is heaven Pappa?" Asked Jamie.
"Well, nobody really knows where heaven is Jamie."
"Why not Jock, it must be somewhere?" Said Clarinda.
"That's one of life's mysteries children, but I know one thing for sure, I know how to get there, oh yes I certainly do."
"In a spaceship." Said Jamie.
"Och see you Jamie, you're aff yir heid." Said Megan.
"It's your spirit that goes to heaven." Said Clarinda.

“That’s right Clarinda, but it’s only good people who get into heaven. That’s why you should never do anybody any harm, or do bad things. Because if you do, they will come back and haunt you in some other way later on in your life, and you will not get to heaven.”
“Is that where all the angels come from Pappa?” Asked Jamie.
“Aye that’s right son.”
“Everybody’s got a guardian angel Jamie.” Said Clarinda.
“Well ah’ve never met mine.” Said Jamie.
“He must be hiding from you Jamie; maybe he knows yir daft.” Said Megan.
“Very funny Megan.” Said Jamie.
“Right that’ll do, stop arguing, it’s time yous were in your sleeping bags.” Said Jock.
“Pappa, can we sleep outside the tent so we can watch the stars?” Asked Megan.
“Of course you can, that’s why we are here.” Said Jock.

As they started to settle down for the night, Jock thought, what a good day it had been. He had thoroughly enjoyed himself and so had the kids. One by one they slowly fell asleep, safe in the arms of the sandman, underneath the stars. Luath snuggled into Megan’s sleeping bag just as she had fallen asleep.

Jock woke up early in the morning and started to make the breakfast. After they had their bacon and eggs they broke camp and started for home. When Jamie and Megan got home they started to tell their Mum all about their first night sleeping under the stars.

“Aye, it was great Mam.” Said Megan. “I saw three shooting stars.”
“I hope you made a wish Megan.”
“Oh yes Mum, but I’m not telling anybody.” Said Megan.
“It was fantastic Mam.” Said Jamie. “Ah’m goin’ up the hills tae live Mam.”
“Aye so you are Jamie.” Said Maggie. “How are you going to survive son?”
“Well, Ah can live aff the land, nae bother, and eat rabbits and pheasants.”
Maggie decided to keep him going.
“And what will you do for water and heating Jamie?”
“Ah’ll get watter fae McKinneys Well, and sleep in ma sleeping bag.” Said Jamie.
“Where will you get money from son?”
“Ah don’t need money, the American Indians didn’y need money, and ne’ther did the Aborigines.”
“So when are you moving up the hills Jamie?” Asked Maggie.
“The morra.”
“Who with?” Said Maggie, holding her laugh in.
“Joost m’self, I’ll take Luath, he can catch the rabbits.”
“How’re ye going to catch the pheasants son?”
“Wi’ ma bow n’ arra, nae bother Mam.”

“Here’s Megan coming, tell her what you are doing.”
“I’m going up the hills to stay Megan.” Said Jamie.
“Och he’s bananas Mam, don’t listen to him.” Said Megan.
“Are you wanting a lift up to your campsite Jamie?” Said Maggie.
“Och it’s alright Mam, I’ll walk up and set up camp at McKinneys Well, Ah want tae be independent.” Said Jamie.
“Ah’ll independence you the noo, git awa’ up they stairs and into that toilet and get yirself washed, ya wee dreamer that you are.” Said Maggie.
Maggie chased Jamie up the stairs, skelping his bum as they all started to laugh. Jamie turned round at the top of the stairs and shouted.
“Aye, yees awe think I’m daft, wance ah’m bigger me and Luath are shootin’ the craw (disappearing), ha ha ha.”

Chapter 12

The Trip To Tam o' Shanter Land

July 21st

It was the morning of the twenty first of July 1996, the 200th anniversary of the death of Robert Burns. Jock had promised the children that he would take them down to Alloway in Ayr to see the birthplace of the Bard. Burns had died in Dumfries, but that was a wee bit too far for the kids to travel. Especially Clarinda, but one day he would take them there to see the Poet's grave.

Megan and Jamie had arrived at Clarinda's house, and they were all sitting waiting patiently on Robin Redbreast making an appearance. Clarinda lifted her hand and opened it and started to whistle. Then all of a sudden Robin landed on the table chirping. Clarinda had told Megan and Jamie to sit very still and not to say anything. Robin Redbreast jumped up on to Clarinda's hand and started to eat the crushed cornflakes. Jamie and Megan were smiling with their eyes wide open.
"Be still Megan, you too Luath." Clarinda whispered.
Before Robin Redbreast had finished eating out of Clarinda's hand he suddenly flew on to Megan's shoulder. Megan froze, and then he flew back to Clarinda's hand.
"He likes you Megan." Said Clarinda.
Then Robin Redbreast flew back up to the holly tree, for he must have sensed Maggie and Jock arriving. Jock walked into the garden, and after a few words with Clarinda's parents he said.
"C'mon kids, let's go, we've got a train to catch."

They arrived at the Central Station with half an hour to spare before the ten o' clock train down to Ayr. They all sat in the centre of the station looking up at the roof and watching the people as they waited on their trains, fascinated. The kids were mesmerised, as this was their first time in a railway station and their first train ride.
"Just imagine." Said Jock. "All the famous people that have walked through this railway station since it was opened in the last century."
"There must have been millions Pappa." Said Megan.
"Aye, and all the people who went to war and didn'y return. People emigrating, people running away, murderers, spies and people going on holiday, film stars and royalty, and pop groups." Said Jock.
"Huv the Spice Girls been through here Pappa?" Asked Jamie.

“Och see you and they Spice Girls Jamie, yir aff yir heid, so ye ur.” Said Megan.
“Right that’ll do yous two, lets go for the train.” Said Jock.

As the train slowly pushed it’s way out of Glasgow Central the kids sat in silence staring out the windows. They passed over the River Clyde where thousands of ships were born.
“What’s that river called Pappa?” Asked Jamie.
“That’s the wonderful Clyde Jamie, the Clyde was one of the most busiest shipbuilding rivers in the world at one time. And Glasgow was the second city of the British Empire.”
“What was the first?” Asked Megan.
“London.” Said Clarinda.
“That’s correct.” Said Jock.

About five minutes later the ticket inspector arrived.
“Tickets please.”
Jock handed the tickets to him. The inspector said, as he winked at Jock.
“By jings that’s a lovely dog, hello boy.” He bent down to clap Luath and Luath started to growl.
“Oh what’s the matter with him?” Said the inspector.
“He doesn’t like uniforms inspector, he had a bad experience with a postman when he was young.”Said Jock.
“Och that’s a shame, he’s a lovely looking dog, I like that star on his forehead. Mind and look after him.”
“We will.” Said Megan.
“What’s his name?” Asked the inspector.
“Luath” Said Jamie.
“He’s named after Robert Burns’s dog, who was also called Luath.” Said Clarinda.
“And what do you know about Robert Burns, what’s your name?” Asked the inspector.
“My name is Clarinda.”

The inspector was taken aback, for he had not expected such an answer.
“I think you have made a big mistake asking Clarinda about Robert Burns.” Said Jock, with a huge grin on his face.
“And who was Clarinda?” The inspector said.
“Clarinda was a pseudonym for a Lady called Nancy McElhose, a lady Robert Burns was in love with. And his pseudonym was ‘Sylvander.’ Rabbie wrote ‘Ae Fond Kiss’ for her. Is there anything else you would like to know?” Said Clarinda, with a nice smile.
“No, I think I’ve met my match Clarinda, it’s been nice meeting yous.” Said the inspector, as he moved away.
The kids started to laugh, and so did Jock.
“Aye you sorted him oot Clarinda.” Said Megan.

Then Jamie said, right out of the blue.
"Hey Pappa, whit does Dumfries mean?"
"I don't know son, what do you think it means Jamie?"
Jamie thought for a few moments, then said.
"A know whit it means Pappa." Said Jamie.
"What?" Said Megan.
"Daft Chips." Said Jamie, as he burst out laughing.
"Aye that's a good one Jamie." Said Jock.
"He's crackers." Said Megan.

About twenty minutes later after they had left Paisley, they were travelling down the west coast of Alba (Scotland). It was a beautiful day with not a cloud in the sky, as Jock pointed out all the different sights. There was the Isle of Bute and Ailsa Craig, and Prestwick airport. And the many golf courses all down that beautiful west coast of Caledonia. 'Oh yes, what a lovely country we live in, people should be proud to live in such a place.' Thought Jock.

They arrived at Ayr Station at eleven o' clock and walked out to Robert Burns Statue Square, to catch the wee bus that would take them down to Alloway Cottage, the birthplace of the Bard.

They spent a good hour in the museum, but Jock knew that to see and read everything in the museum you would have to spend, not just one hour, but about a hundred. While they were in the museum Clarinda lifted a Tam o' Shanter tartan bonnet and tried it on, she really looked great.
"You suit that Clarinda." Said Megan.
"Thank you Megan." Said Clarinda, as she walked to the mirror and smiled at herself.
Two seconds later Jamie was wearing a Tam o' Shanter, and said.
"Can I get one Pappa, please?"
"Aye, alright, you can all get one." Ach well, thought Jock it was the kids' day out, and he didn't want them to forget it.

And then they all started to walk down to Alloway churchyard. As the kids walked in front of Jock he thought. 'My God look at they weans, they look great, aye, and so happy.' As the kids walked on in front of him laughing and skipping, he saw Megan take Clarinda's hand, like a big sister. Jock thought how lovely that was because Megan knew that Clarinda was not well, and Megan would always be there for Clarinda, that's what true friends were for, forever. Jock could hear the kids singing.

"We are the Crambo Clinkers,
We make rhymes up everyday,
We are the Crambo Clinkers'
We're doon at Ayr for the day"

As they stood in front of the grave of William Burness, Jock said.
"That's Robert Burns father who is buried there."
"That's a bit stupid that Pappa." Said Jamie.
"See you Jamie, yir no' real, remember we are in a graveyard." Said Megan.
"What dae you mean Jamie?" Said Jock.
"They've spelt' his name wrang Pappa."
"No they haven't, that was his real name, Mr Burness changed his name when he moved down to Ayrshire." Said Clarinda.
"That's correct Clarinda very good." Said Jock.
While they were talking Luath walked over to William Burness's headstone and lifted his leg.
"Oh my God Luath, you bad boy, that's terrible, peeing on a grave." Said Megan.
"Right that's it, let's go." Said Jock. But inside Jock was laughing, and he knew that Burns would have laughed as well.

After they had seen the Tam o' Shanter film, they walked over to the Brig o' Doon to take some photographs. Then they decided to walk back up in to Ayr as it was a nice day. By the time they got to Robert Burns Square they were all starving.
"Who wants a fish supper?" Shouted Jock.
"Me, me, me." The kids shouted.
"Ah'm starvin' Pappa, a' could eat a wudden dumplin', so a could." Said Jamie.
"Och see him Clarinda, don't listen to him, he thinks he's funny." Said Megan.

And so they got their fish suppers and walked over to the train station for a seat before the train came. As they sat eating their fish suppers Luath sat patiently waiting on a chip or even a bit of fish. He would wink with both eyes alternately, and sit on his back legs with his front paws in a begging position. Passers-by would stop and look and laugh, as Luath performed. For he was the star of the show, as were the kids. Jock asked a lady if she would take some pictures of them, and then they all got on the train and headed home.

That night Jock had a few beers with his drouthy cronies in the Auld Hoose. Later on as he lay in bed he thought. 'What a lovely day it has been today, it's a pity every day could not be like that. But that's the way life goes, some days are good, other days not so good, and some absolutely murder polis. You just play the cards you are dealt in the game of life and hope for the best.'

Chapter 13

Burnt Toast and Oaringes

About four weeks later near the end of August, Maggie woke up about six o' clock one morning with an uneasy feeling. She knew something was wrong, a cold shiver ran down the back of her neck. She got up and walked straight into Jamies room, he was there, then she went into Megan's room, she was there, but Luath was gone, strange, she thought. She went back into Jamies room and walked over and lifted the quilt, no Jamie, he had put his pillows under the quilt to make it look as though he was there. He was Vincent Van Gogh (off), as he said he would be one day. Maggie started to panic, she ran down the stairs thinking Jamie would be there, but he wasn't, Jamie was off. She searched everywhere then she phoned Jock.

"He's definitely not here Dad, I've checked everywhere, even the garden hut. His sleeping bag and his haversack have gone, he's even cleaned out the fridge, and tins of dog meat are missing as well."
"Don't panic Maggie, at least we know he's not been kidnapped. He's got Luath with him, so he will be all right."
"It's alright saying that Dad, but he's only eight, where will he have gone, I'm so worried." Said Maggie.
"He's probably away up the Three Steps to where we were camping, don't worry, I'll go up there right away."

It started to rain as Jock was walking through the Campsie golf course, the quickest way to the Three Steps. He arrived at the campsite half an hour later, but there was no sign of Jamie. Jock started to get concerned. The rain began to get heavier and then Jock decided to walk down to the Redwood Tree; maybe Jamie would be there. A wee while later as Jock was approaching the Redwood Tree he could see smoke starting to rise, Jock's heart lifted, for he knew that it would be Jamie trying to light a fire. Thank God he thought. 'What a boy he is.'

The moment Jock saw Jamie he decided not to get on to him and give him a row, for he knew that Jamie would turn against him if he did. Jock believed that you had to talk to kids and let them know that you cared, and also to give them the respect that they deserved because of their innocence. For that was the way that Jock had been brought up, but sometimes you had to be a wee bit firm with them.

But there were ways and means of educating children, instead of shouting at them or raising your hands to them.

As Jock was walking down the wee path to the Redwood Tree, Jamie turned and saw him coming.
"Hi Pappa." Said Jamie, it was as if he had done nothing wrong.
"Hello there Jamie, how's it goin'?"
"A canny get this fire tae light Pappa."
"Och nae wonder, yir sticks are wet, wait and I'll show you son."

So Jock showed Jamie how to light a fire, and in no time at all it was blazing.
"Are ye wantin' something to eat Pappa?" Said Jamie, with not a care in the world. Jock burst out laughing, he couldn't help it.
"Whit ur ye laughing at Pappa?"
"I'm laughing at you Jamie, you are not real, you're unbelievable son."
"Wee boys who are eight years old are not supposed to run away you know."
"Och a know Pappa, but ah knew you would find me anyway."
"Your mother is very upset you know." Said Jock quietly.
"I know, I'm sorry Pappa."
"Your ma best pal Jamie, aren't you?"
"I sure am Pappa."
"Well you're also my grandson, and I am responsible for bringing you up, and Megan as well. I'm trying to teach you good manners and how to be a good person, and educate you all about life, is that not right Jamie?"
"Aye that's right Pappa." Said Jamie, as he walked over to his Pappa. Jock put his arms out and lifted Jamie up and they started to cuddle each other, then Jamie started to cry.

"It's alright Jamie, you're a good boy, and you are ma best pal in the whole wide world."
"Ah'm so sorry Pappa, ah'll never run away again."
"Right son it's okay, let's get your stuff together and get back to my house and phone your mother." Said Jock.

"Well thank God you found him Dad, that boy is drivin' me up the wa', so he is."
"Ach he's joost at that age Maggie, he thinks he's old enough to do anything. He's got so much confidence, which can't be a bad thing." Said Jock.
"I think I'll have to put a lock on his door Dad."
"Don't be daft Maggie, listen, let Jamie and Megan come doon tae ma hoose and stay the night. I'll have a good talk to them, I'll give them burnt toast and oaringees tonight, they'll love it."
"Well alright Dad, somehow I don't think Jamie will run away from you."

So a wee while later Megan, Jamie, Jock and Luath were walking past Clarinda's house. They knocked on the door but there was no one in, and so they proceeded to Jock's house. Jock had made totties and mince, and every time that particular dish was made the plates were licked clean.
"That wus smashin' Pappa, when ur we getting the burnt toast 'n oaringees'?" Said Jamie.
"Later on, once yous have helped to clean out the fire, chop fire sticks and get some coal in. Then once the fire is really hot, we'll burn the toast."

After they lit the fire and Megan had done the dishes they went for a wee walk down to the Redwood Tree. When they returned the fire was roaring. Jock told the kids to go and sit by the fire while he went to the scullery. He returned with six slices of square bread and three oranges and some Lurpak butter. He took a slice of bread and stuck it on to a long fork and held it up to the flames of the fire. Within seconds the bread was burnt, then he turned it round and burnt the other side. The kids were amazed.

Jock handed the toast to Megan who buttered it immediately. They all took a piece of toast and a slice of orange. Jock says.
"Right kids, take a bite of toast then a bite of orange."
Megan and Jamie started to eat, and they loved it.
Luath looked on, his mouth watering watching them, and his eyes begging and winking.
"Awe Pappa, that's brilliant." Said Megan.
"Smashin'." Said Jamie.
"I told yous that you would like it."
"I wish Clarinda was here to taste it, I wonder why she wasn't in." Said Megan.

And so the burnt toast and oaringees were devoured, then Megan and Jamie washed the dishes and tidied up the scullery. Luath sat staring up at Jamie as he dried the dishes.
"See that Luath Pappa, he's no' real he eats fish, he eats oaringees, he even ate a an onion and a banana, a' think he's hauf human."
"Aye, I think yir right son." Said Jock.

Just then the phone rang. Megan answered it.
"It's for you Pappa, it's Mr Brady."
Jock took the phone from Megan. His first thought was, that something was wrong here, he just had a funny feeling. He looked into Megan's eyes, and she looked concerned.
"Hello John, how you doin'? Fine thanks, oh no, is she alright, right I will, okay, cheers, maybe see you tomorrow John, yes I will, goodnight."
"Clarinda has been taken into Yorkhill Hospital." Said Jock.

"Oh no." Said Megan. "What happened, is she alright Pappa?"
"She's alright, she just wasn't feeling too good, so don't worry about it."
"She needs a new kidney Pappa doesn't she?" Said Megan.
"Aye she does Megan, let's hope she gets one soon, we'll all say prayers for her tonight to help her." Said Jock.
"Ah pray for Clarinda every night Pappa, she's ma best pal. Before ah ran away she told me not to go, but a didn'y listen and she didn'y tell anybody, that's why she's ma best pal." Said Jamie.
"Aye she's a lovely wee lassie, you're both lucky to have a friend like Clarinda." Said Jock.
"Aye so we are." Said Megan.

Later on Jamie and Megan said goodnight to Jock. Then before they got into the bed couch they both knelt down and said some prayers for Clarinda. Luath knelt down beside them with his head between his two paws as if he was praying as well, well, maybe he was.

After prayers they jumped into bed and Luath snuggled in beside them. Jamie said.
"Megan do you think Clarinda will be alright?"
"Of course she will, as soon as she gets a new kidney she will be running faster than you and me."
"Ah hope so, see me Megan, ah'll never run away again, ah've learnt ma lesson. Ah canny even make a bow 'n arra never mind shoot a pheasant."
"Och we all know that Jamie, ah canny imagine Luath catchin' rabbits either. He's not bred for that, he's a sheep dog. So get to sleep, and you better not run away again, or the Polis will catch you and put you in the jail."
"Ach, the Polis don't frighten me Megan."
"Och yir aff yir heid Jamie, joost get tae sleep, and it's ma turn to cuddle into Luath, goodnight." Said Megan.

And as the kids fell asleep, Jock was thinking that it hadn't been a very good day today, but the children had to learn all about life and had to take the good with the bad. Jamie had learned his lesson and hopefully Clarinda would get better. Please God help Clarinda, she's a lovely wee girl.

Chapter 14

When a Stranger Opens Up

"Och Jamie, look at the state of your hands and face, look at him Pappa, he's eating more brambles than he's collecting." Said Megan.
"Ah love brambles Pappa." Said Jamie.
"I've told you before Jamie, don't eat too many or you will get a sore stomach." Said Jock.
They were collecting brambles to make jelly, Jock had made it every year for as long as he could remember, and he loved it. They were away up past the South Braes near the auld Drover's road, and as Jock looked at Jamie and Megan, in his mind's eye he could see himself fifty years ago, picking brambles with his auld grannie Nelly McKinnie and his mother and father.

'How time flies.' Thought Jock. 'It seemed like, one minute you were a young child and then you were sixty years old. How swiftly the time beats for every human being. That's why Jock could never understand, why people argued fussed and fought with one another, and worried about this and that and the next thing. What is the point? Life is far too short. And all these people who have millions of pounds in the bank, and the people who make money their God, well they will find out someday that it does not mean a thing. What Jock was doing right now, could not be bought. Out in the fresh air in the countryside picking brambles with his grandchildren.
But fifty years! Where did it go?'

"Right kids, c'mon and sit down and enjoy the view, and we'll have some sandwiches." Said Jock.
They sat on the crest of a hill and lay back in the sun. It was a beautiful September morning with a clear sky and not a breath of wind. Away over to the east lay Kilsyth and Cumbernauld.
"If I had brought my binoculars we would have been able to see the Forth Road Bridge." Said Jock.
"That's next to the Forth Railway Bridge Pappa, isn't it?" Said Jamie.
"Aye that's right son, they are quite near Edinburgh, and what's the nickname of Edinburgh?"
"I know." Said Megan.
"It's Auld Reekie." Said Jamie.
"But why is it called Auld Reekie?"
"Because of the smoke comin' oot the chimneys." Said Jamie.

"Well done Jamie, and what was the name of the wee dog in that film you saw, that was filmed in Edinburgh?" Asked Jock.
"Greyfriars Bobby." Said Jamie, with a big smile, as he cuddled Luath.
"Well done Jamie, they brambles must be good for your brains." Said Jock.

Megan changed the subject.
"My basket is nearly full Pappa."
"That's great Megan, I think we'll huv tae help Jamie fill his."
"Aye, there are more brambles in his stomach than in his basket."
"Very funny Megan, Luath has eaten a lot of my brambles." Said Jamie.
"Aye right Jamie, don't blame Luath, it's you that's been feeding him." Said Megan.
"Oh, but honest Pappa, every time a turn ma back, or put ma basket doon, that Luath eats ma brambles, he's a wee fox. Look at him sitting there looking so innocent, he knows we are talking about him." Said Jamie.
"Right, stop arguing you two, let's get the baskets filled."

"Are we going into Yorkhill hospital to see Clarinda Pappa?"
"Yes Megan, we'll go in later this afternoon."
"She would have loved to have been with us today, wouldn't she Pappa?" Said Megan.
"Aye she would have Megan, you can tell her all about it later."
"Do you think Clarinda will be alright Pappa?" Asked Jamie.
"I hope tae God she is son."
"Aye, well, a just hope she is and God answers ma prayers, cos if he disny, am no gon tae Mass again." Said Jamie.
"You shouldn't say that Jamie, you can't blame God for everything."
"Sometimes your prayers don't get answered." Said Jock.
"How no?" Asked Jamie, looking bewildered.
"Because eh, because." Jock was a wee bit lost for words. "Well let me tell yous a wee story about this man I once met."

"A few years ago I was walking up the Campsie Fells, and I met this guy at the very top. And when you meet someone at the top of the hills you don't just walk past them, you say hello and have a wee blether with them. Now remember this man was a total stranger to me. We started talking about the weather about life and this and that. And after about five minutes we started to talk about religion, and about how he did not believe in God anymore.
He had prayed to God and it had not helped him, he just believed that you were born, you lived, and then you died, and that was that."
"Why was he like that Pappa?" Asked Megan.
"Well, there was a reason for the way he felt. His son was killed in a car crash in Canada, and that is why he was so angry and bitter about God."

“That’s terrible Pappa, it’s a shame.” Said Jamie.
“Aye, and I could understand the man’s feelings, it was his only son and he was only twenty one. You see kids, God works in mysterious ways, and even though your prayers don’t get answered you must have faith. When God decides to take you from this life there’s nothing we can do about it. So, don’t ever lose your faith, keep praying for Clarinda and she will be alright.”
“Look at Luath Pappa, he’s fast asleep.” Said Megan.
“He’s not real, right Luath let’s get going, it’s time to make the bramble jelly.”

Later on that afternoon they all went in to Yorkhill hospital. As they were walking into the ward Clarinda was sitting up reading a book, but she looked a wee bit pale. Megan and Jamie told her all about the day they had picking brambles and having a picnic. Clarinda was putting on a brave face, but deep inside she was desperate to be out of the hospital, healthy and running about with her friends. A wee while later as Megan was giving Clarinda a wee cuddle before they left, something caught her eye at the window.
“Look! What’s that at the window?”
Everybody turned their heads.
“It’s Robin Redbreast.” Said Clarinda.
“So it is, he’s followed you into the hospital Clarinda, that’s amazing.” Said Megan.
Then all of a sudden Clarinda’s face was beaming and everybody was smiling; maybe Clarinda’s luck was going to change, and if anybody deserved a change of luck it was Clarinda.
So they all said their farewells.

As Jamie and Megan and their Pappa were walking out of the hospital, Jamie said.
“Pappa, do you think that was the real Robin Redbreast from Clarinda’s garden?”
Jock did not hesitate with his answer.
“You better believe it Jamie, that’s him alright, that’s Clarinda’s Robin Redbreast.”
“That’s amazing Pappa, they robins are very clever, aren’t they?” Said Jamie.
“Aye, flying all the way from Campsie, nae bother.” Said Jock.

Later on that night Jock had showed the kids how to make bramble jelly, then he took them home to their Mum’s. On the way Megan went into Clarinda’s and gave her mother a jar of bramble jelly. She told Mrs Brady all about all about the hospital visit and seeing Robin Redbreast. Mrs Brady said.
“That’s quite strange Megan, ever since Clarinda went into the hospital Robin Redbreast has not been seen here.”
“Oh my God! that must be him right enough at the hospital, that Jamie said that it might not be him, wait till I tell Pappa, see you later Mrs Brady.”
“Goodbye Megan.”

That night Jock went to the Auld Hoose for a couple of beers, all the boys were there, Auld Duncan and Thomas and Safari Sam.
"How's Luath getting on Jock?" Asked Safari.
"Och, he's great thanks Sam."
"Aye he's a bonny dog Jock, I seen the weans wi' him the other day, he looks great."
"Cheers Sam."

As Jock lay in his bed that night he thought.
'Aye it's been a good day, but it was strange about Robin Redbreast. He had told his friends in the pub what had happened and they all thought the same. Auld Duncan had said that Jimmy the Jeiner worked in mysterious ways.'

And so Jock fell in to the arms of the Sandman as night fell on Auld Campsie Toun. The honest men and bonnie lasses were going about their lawful business, well some of them anyway.

Chapter 15

When Prayers Are Answered

And so the days and the weeks flew by, and Jock and the kids were still going in to visit Clarinda every other day. Every morning and at night before Jamie and Megan went to bed they would kneel down and say their prayers for Clarinda. Even Luath prayed, he would sit next to Jamie or Megan with his paws together as if he knew what was happening. Megan had taken photographs of Luath in to the hospital to show to Clarinda, who says that she was desperate to see Luath and to go for long walks.

Near the end of October Jock and the kids were down at the Redwood tree, when out of the blue Jamie says.
"Hey Pappa."
"What is it son?"
"Ah'll huv tae write a letter tae God."
"What for Jamie."
"Tae ask God tae make Clarinda better." Said Jamie.
Jock thought, this could be interesting.
"Okay then Jamie, when we get back to my house, you can write tae God."
And so half an hour later they sat down at Jock's big dining table, Jock handed Jamie the pen and paper and said.
"Right Jamie, write away son."
"What will I write Pappa?"
"Well you are the one that wants to write, so carry on." Said Jock.

Jamie wrote down his address and then the date and said.
"Dear God, na, that disn'y sound right Pappa, whit's God's first name?"
"It's Jimmy, Jimmy the Jeiner (joiner)." Said Jock.
"Jimmy the Jeiner, how did he get that name."
"Well, it's a nickname, you know how Jesus was a carpenter?"
"Aye."
"Well a carpenter is a joiner, it's the same thing."
"Is that because he tries to join people together Pappa."
"Aye, well you've got a good point there son, that's maybe right enough." 'This wee boy isn'y daft.' Thought Jock. 'The things children say.'
"Right then Jamie on you go start writing, Megan and me will go and get the dinner ready'."
About ten minutes later Jamie handed the letter to Jock and he read it out to Megan.

Dear Jimmy The Jeiner,

I hope this letter finds you and Jesus and all your family well. My name is Jamie Mackenzie, I am a Cafflic and go to chapel every Sunday. I am a good boy, except for the time me and Luath ran awa' up the hills. A will never dae that again, honest. Ma best pal Clarinda is in the hospital and she needs a new kidney. Please, please could you get her one and make her better.

Thank you God,
And cheerio the noo
Jamie Mackenzie.

"That's a good letter Jamie." Said Megan.
"Thanks Megan, have you got an envelope Pappa?"
"Aye here's one son." Said Jock.
"Whit's Jimmy the Jeiners address Pappa?"
"Eh, Jimmy the Jeiner, Paradise, Heaven." Said Jock.
"Whit's the postcode?"
"Eh, GOD NO.1." Said Jock.
"Right Pappa, we better get up the street right away and get this posted."
"Right okay kids, let's go."

When they reached the postbox Jamie put the letter to his lips and kissed it. He then let Megan and Jock kiss it. He made the sign of the cross, and as he dropped the letter into the box, the bell at St Machans sounded at exactly six o'clock. They all looked at each other in surprised silence.
"Is that not the strangest thing, just as you dropped the letter into the post box 'Mary McQuade' peeled?" Said Jock.
"Who is 'Mary McQuade'?" Asked Megan.
"That's the name of the bell at St Machans."
"How did it get that name Pappa?" Asked Jamie.
"Wait till we get back to the house and I will tell yous all about it." Said Jock.

When they got back to Jock's house he started to tell the kids all about the bell at St Machans.
"In 1935 the Chapel bell at St Machans was taken down for repair because the wooden support had rotted away. It had been there since 1870 when the chapel was built."
"It must be quite heavy." Said Jamie.
"It weighs about 210 kilos, it's made of brass and has risen letters and figures on it. It was made by J Murphy a founder of Dublin, and was gifted to St Machans by a man called John McQuade of Haughhead. The priest at that time was father Magini who was Italian.

There is an inscription on the bell, which reads.

Joannes Macwade De Hauhead.
Donavit MDCCCLXX A.D.

Underneath this are two branches of shamrocks, with three shamrocks to each branch, the branches being crossed over each other, the whole thing being surmounted by an Irish Crown and Harp. The bell has always been known as 'Mary McQuade', after the wife of the donator."

"That's amazing Pappa, but is it not weird that when Jamie put the letter to Jimmy The Jeiner into the post box, Mary McQuade chimed?" Said Megan.
"Aye, that's very strange indeed Megan, very strange." Said Jock
"Maybe God knew that a wus sending him a letter, and that wus his way of lettin' me know, well ma teacher says that God knows everything, so it must be true." Said Jamie.

Later on that night Jock went for a pint to the Auld Hoose. There had been a singsong going on for a wee while and everybody was in a fine mood. Auld Duncan was laughing and joking after somebody had told him a joke. Then his mood suddenly changed and he said.
"Yous probably all remember the Auchengeich Pit disaster, so here's a wee song that you might not have heard."

Everybody looked surprised because auld Duncan had never been known to sing before.
"Right here we go, it's to the tune of 'Skippin' Barfit Thru the Heather', here goes."

In Auchengeich there stands a pit,
The wheel above, it isna turning,
For on a grey September morn',
The flames o' Hell were burnin'.

Though in below the coal lay rich,
It's richer noo, for awe that burning,
For forty seven brave men are deid,
Tae wives and sweethearts,ne'er returning.

The seams are thick in Auchengeich,
The coal below is black and glistening,
But och, it's cost is faur ower dear,
For human lives there is nae reckoning.

Oh coal is black and coal is red,
An' coal is rich beyond a treasure,
It's black wi' work an' red wi' blood,
It's richness noo in lives we measure.

Oh better noo we'd never wrocht,
A thousand years o' work an' grievin',
The coal is black like the mourning shroud,
The women left behind are weaving.

After thunderous applause Jock says.
"That was brilliant Duncan, ah've never heard you singing before."
"Ach, there's a helluva lot of things you don't know about me Jock. One o' ma best pals died in that disaster, Dennis Mcilhaney and another two Campsie men, Andrew McKenna and George McEwan, God bless them all."
"Aye, a terrible tragedy, very sad."
"Aye, thirty seven years ago, how time flies." Said Jock.
"Anyway here's a wee poem a wrote the other day when I was looking in the mirror."

The Mirror Man.

Oh my God,
I'm runnin' oot o' teeth,
A'll huv tae phone up the butcher,
And cancel awe ma beef.

Oh my God,
Ma eyesight's getting worse,
A'll huv tae phone the optician,
Or preferably a nurse.

Oh my God,
Ma hair is fallin' oot,
A'll huv tae phone up the wig man,
Before a look like a coot.

Oh my God,
Am runnin' oot o' beer,
A'll huv tae phone up the brewery,
But it's too bloody dear.

Oh my God
A'm half bloody pissed,
A wud! Phone up God',
But, I'm an atheist.

"Well done Jock, that was good, but that's one thing you are not, you are not an Atheist." Said Duncan.
"Aye, thank God for that Duncan."

The following morning Maggie answered the telephone, it was Mrs Brady.
"Hello Maggie, I've just had a phone call from Yorkhill Hospital, Clarinda has been taken into the operating theatre, she's getting a new kidney today."
"Oh that's fantastic, you must be so happy, I hope everything goes alright for her."
"Thanks Maggie, I'll let you know how she is later on today, Megan and Jamie will be thrilled to bits."
"So they will, they're just getting up for school, see you later Mary."

And so Maggie shouted the good news up the stairs to the kids. They came running down the stairs all excited.
"Is that right Mam, is that right enough?" Asked Megan.
"Aye, aye, she's in the operating theatre right now." Said Maggie.
"A tell't yees God wud answer ma letter, he wus helluva quick wasn't he Mam?"
"Aye son, he sure was, but take your time Jamie, Clarinda's body might not except the kidney, it might not work."
"How no', a kidney's a kidney." Said Jamie.
"But they're all different son, let's just hope that it works."
"Mam that means that somebody has died, and Clarinda is getting their kidney doesn't it?" Said Megan.
"That's possible Megan, but not necessarily true. But sometimes life can be cruel and hopefully Clarinda will get well again. But you must keep praying, there is a long way to go."

A wee while later Megan and Jamie took Luath down to the Redwood Tree and said a couple of prayers for Clarinda. They were both very happy now, and felt sure Clarinda would get better.

Chapter 16

Luath Disappears

Two days later Maggie, Jock and the kids went into Yorkhill to see Clarinda. She did not look great but at least she was smiling and was a lot happier. They were not allowed to stay very long because of Clarinda's condition.

On the way home Megan says.
"Mum, I don't want any Xmas presents this year."
"Why not Megan?"
"Because I want to give all the money to Yorkhill to all the sick children and children in need, because the hospital helped to make Clarinda better."
"That's very kind of you Megan." Said Maggie.
"Me tae Mam, a don't want any presents either, ah'd rether go fur a walk wi' Clarinda." Said Jamie.
"That's very nice of you Jamie." Said Jock.

It was about ten days later that Clarinda got out of the hospital. Everyday she got that wee bit stronger and her smile got that wee bit bigger. As soon as she was home she phoned Megan and Jamie to bring Luath down to see her, and go for a walk down to the Redwood Tree. Clarinda's mother had told her to take her time and she would be able to walk a wee bit further everyday.

On the 30th of November, the birthday of St Andrew, the kids were walking through the Field Park on their way home, when Luath ran into some tall thick bushes near the car park. After shouting and whistling for a few minutes Luath had not come back. The kids walked over to the car park, but Luath was nowhere to be seen. They looked everywhere, but could not find him. They started to get a bit worried.
"Och he's probably roon in the hoose waitin' on us." Said Jamie.
"I don't think so." Said Clarinda. "I've got a bad feeling and I don't like it."
"What do you mean Clarinda?" Asked Megan.
"I don't know Megan, something has happened to Luath. I can feel it, it's weird. Did you not see that white van that left the car park?" Said Clarinda.
"No." Said Megan.
"Ah seen a white van Clarinda." Said Jamie.
"Surely nobody would steal Luath away?" Said Megan, almost in tears.

They looked and shouted for another ten minutes, but Luath was gone, Megan says.
"Quick Jamie, you run and get Pappa, maybe Luath is at his house. Tell Pappa to phone Mum and see if Luath is home, quick hurry up."
"Right Megan, yous stay here in case Luath comes back."

Jamie ran as fast as he could, and when he got to his Pappa's house he turned the handle and banged on the door. His Pappa was not in. 'Oh no.' Thought Jamie, 'Where is he? I know, The Auld Hoose.' He ran to the pub and went straight in through the swing doors like a miniature John Wayne. He knew where his Pappa sat, so he went into the lounge. Jock was sitting with his friends. Jamie shouted.
"Pappa, Pappa, Luath's disappeared, he's been stolen."

"Now calm doon son, whit's happened?" Said Jock.
Jamie told his Pappa what had happened, about Luath going into the bushes and the white van.
"Aye, there's been a lot of dogs disappearing lately Jock." Said Safari Sam.
"Ach the swine's that they are, c'mon Jamie let's go son." Said Jock.

Jock phoned Maggie and Luath was not there, and so they hurried from the pub down to the car park to meet Megan and Clarinda. Megan ran to Jock as he approached and Jock lifted her up in to his arms. Megan started to cry.
"Pappa, Pappa somebody has stolen Luath." The tears were running down Megan's cheeks. Then Jamie started to cry, then Clarinda walked over and started to cuddle Megan and Jamie, then Jock put his arms round the three of them and he started to cry.
"Don't you worry kids, we'll get Luath back, the dirty rotten bastards that they are. Now c'mon kids stop crying, you never know, maybe Luath is round at the house waiting on us."
"How can anybody steal somebody's dog Pappa?" Asked Jamie.
"There are a lot of bad people out there son, but don't worry we'll get Luath back."

And so they all started to walk home, two wee girls a wee boy and their Pappa, missing, was Luath their best pal. Then right out of the blue Jamie says.
"Life's a bitch Pappa, isn't it?"
Clarinda and Megan laughed at Jamie's statement.
"Aye, yir right enough son, sometimes it can be."

When they got back to Maggies, Jock phoned the police. About half an hour later a local constable turned up. Clarinda told him all about the white van.
"Did you get the number of the van?" Asked the officer.
"No, it happened too quickly, but I just know that Luath was put into that van, even though I didn't see it." Said Clarinda.
"How do you know if you did not see it?" Asked the policeman, puzzled.

"If Clarinda says it happened it's the truth, cos she knows, and ah seen the van tae." Said Jamie.
"What type of van was it, was it big or small?"
"Ah know! It was wan o' they ex Post Office vans." Said Jamie.
"That's right." Said Clarinda.

The policeman said that he would look into the disappearance of Luath. As he was leaving the house he says.
"Try not to worry kids, we'll do all we can to get Luath back."
"Aye, yees better." Said Jamie.
The officer laughed, and Maggie says.
"Don't you be cheeky Jamie, that's not nice."
"Sorry Mam." Said Jamie.

In the next few days Jock had gone to all the local farms, and checked with the dog warden. But it was now obvious that Luath had been stolen. About four days after Luath had been taken, Maggie phoned Jock.
"Hi Dad, the kids are taking the loss of Luath quite bad, they're not sleeping right not eating properly and they have to be forced to go to school. Can you not get them another dog?"
"No chance Maggie, they want Luath back and that's that. So don't worry we'll get him back. All the guys in the pub know what's happened and sooner or later we will find out who did it."
"But what if we don't get Luath back?"
"Well, we will cross that bridge when we get to it, stop worrying Maggie."
"Right Dad, okay."
"By the way Maggie, I was talking to John, Clarinda's father, and he says that Luath is bred off champion Border collies and has a good pedigree and cost quite a bit of money. Apparently John's cousin has a sheep farm up near Stirling and he was going to get Luath trained."
"Do you think that was the reason he was stolen Dad?"
"Aye it's a possibility."
"Right, okay Dad, I'll tell the kids, I don't think Luath will come to any harm then."
"No, no way Maggie, I'll see you tomorrow."
"Right, 'bye Dad."

Maggie told the kids that Luath was bred from champions.
"Och a knew that Mam, that's obvious, that dug's a star." Said Jamie.
"Aye but we haven't got him, he's our dog." Said Megan.
Megan buried her head in the pillows on the couch and started to sob. Jamie went over and gave her a wee cuddle.
"Don't you worry Megan, am writing anither letter tae God, he'll help us to get Luath back." Said Jamie.

Chapter 17

December 24th, Xmas Eve

Jock had just passed the big house on the hill just after the Campsie Golf Club. A wee rabbit ran out on to the road and up into the gardens of the house on the hill. The chaffinches were dancing through the hawthorns, as were the blue tits and the blackbirds. Then Jock saw a wee goldcrest, which was quite unusual, for they were quite scarce. Then up near McKinney's well he saw two yellow wagtails, maybe that was luck, for every time Jock saw the yellow wagtails he was lucky.

It was a cold day but it was nice and sunny as Jock stared away over to the Dumbarton hills. He thought about the kids, Luath and then his 'Highland Mary', and that made him sad. Christmas day tomorrow, acht well, it was gonny be a rotten Xmas for the weans without Luath, but they just had to get on with life, these things happened.

It was about an hour later as Jock was walking towards his house that he saw auld Duncan emerging from the Auld Hoose.
"Jock come here, quick." Shouted Duncan.
Jock crossed the road.
"Hi Duncan how're ye?"
"C'mon in for a pint, Safari Sam has got something to tell you."
As soon as they got in to the pub Sam says to Jock.
"I think I saw your Luath Jock, I'm almost certain it was him."
"Where, where about Sam?" Said Jock all excited.
"Joost ootside Callander at this guy's house, he's got all sorts of dogs, fighting dugs bulldugs and greyhounds, all sorts."
"Was Luath alright Sam, but how do you know it was Luath, there's thousands of border collies?"
"It was the star on his head Jock, this guys daughter had him on a lead, and I said to my mate Tony, that that dog looks like Luath. The dog heard me and started to pull the girl towards me, that's when I knew it was definitely Luath."
"Who is this guy." Said Jock.
"His name is Mullen, he's supposed to be one o' these hard men fae Glasgow, you know, they move out to the country and they think that the locals are all walking about with straw in their ears."
"I know the type." Said auld Duncan.
"Can you show me where this guy lives Sam?" Said Jock.

"Aye nae bother Jock, it's all arranged, Thomas said he would drive us up, cos I knew when I told you, you would be desperate to go up there."
"I'll phone my son Douglas up to meet us at Callender, you never know we might need him." Said Duncan.

It was almost dark when they arrived at the house. Jock and the boys had met Douglas at the outskirts of Callender and they had proceeded to Mullen's house.

Douglas had done a bit of homework on Mr Mullen while he had waited on Jock and the boys. It seemed that Mullen was a very shifty character indeed and was connected to some hoodlums from Glasgow.

As they walked to the front door of the house a young girl came walking round from the back garden with a border collie on a lead.
Jock shouted immediately.
"Luath! Luath boy."
It was Luath.
Luath ran towards Jock pulling the young girl with him.
He started to whine and bark as Jock clapped and cuddled him.
"Och it's alright Luath, it's alright, och ah love you so."
The tears were running down Jock's face.
Then the door of the house opened and Mullen stepped outside shouting.
"What the hell is going on here?"
Jock turned and shouted.
"You stole ma grandchildren's dug ya bastard."
Jock let Luath go and ran towards Mullen, but Thomas and Sam held him back.
After a few questions Douglas asked Jock if he wanted to press charges.
"No, I wont press charges, not only has Mr Mullen upset my grandchildren he has also upset his own daughter, look at the poor wee lassie crying. But if he admits that he stole Luath I'll definitely not charge him."
"I did steal your dog, okay?" Said Mullen.
One second later Mullen was lying flat on the deck. Auld Duncan was so quick that hardly anybody noticed. A flashing right hook and Mullen was out cold.
"Och Dad, why'd you do that?" Said Sergeant Douglas MacGregor.
"He's lucky that's all he's getting, and ye canny arrest your Dad, can you son?" Said auld Duncan laughing.

Five minutes later Jock and the boys were heading back down the road to Auld Campsie Toun. Jock was so happy as he sat in the back of the car with Luath. It was gonny be a good Xmas now he thought.
"That was some right hook Duncan." Said Thomas.
"Aye they didn'y call me one hit MacGregor for nothin', when a was in the army." Said Duncan.
"Aye well done." Said Sam.

“Aye, you’ll be going for a pint.” Said Duncan.
“No thanks I don’t want to leave Luath by himself after what he’s been through, we’ll have a drink over Xmas boys, I’m buying, and anyway I’m invited round to Maggies for Xmas dinner tomorrow at twelve o’ clock. I canny wait tae see their faces when they see Luath.”
“What a surprise Jock, that’s brilliant.”Said Duncan.
“Aye it’s gonny be a good Xmas now Luath.” Said Jock.

Christmas Day

It was ten minutes to twelve when Jock and Luath left the house, Jock said.
"Well Luath, I think we'll have to go in and see Clarinda first, after all, you really do belong to her."
Jock rang the bell at Clarinda's house, he heard Clarinda skipping along the wooden floor towards the door. She opened the door.
For two seconds she was speechless.
"Luath! Luath oh my Luath, my God."
Clarinda was cuddling Luath and crying, then Mr and Mrs Brady appeared. Jock told them what had happened. After a few minutes Jock said.
"I better go Clarinda, will you be going for a walk after Xmas dinner."
"Och Jock, you do ask silly questions, of course I'll be going. Tell Megan and Jamie to phone me, they will be so happy, see you later Jock."

On the way to Maggies Luath started to pull Jock quite hard.
"Ach take yir time Luath."
Three minutes later they were walking up Maggies garden path. Jamie happened to look out the window. He couldn't believe his eyes. He shouted to Megan.
"It's Pappa Megan, quick, quick, a think he's got Luath."
"Aye right Jamie."
But Megan jumped from the couch, and they both ran and opened the door.
Jock let Luath off the lead.
The kids ran on to the porch.
Luath was barking and whining.
Megan and Jamie were ecstatic, and they started to shout.
"Luath, oh Luath, it's Luath, oh Pappa."
Luath ran on to the front garden.
Megan and Jamie ran after him.
Then they were rolling about in the snow cuddling Luath and each other. They started to cry and then they would laugh then they would cry again. Then Maggie cuddled Jock and she started to cry.
"Och Dad I'm so happy, it's gonny be some Xmas now."

After all the excitement they all calmed down and Jock told them all about how he found Luath.
"Ah knew you would find him Pappa, ah just knew it." Said Jamie.
Megan usually answered anything Jamie said, but she was so happy she just let it pass.
"Mum." Said Megan.
"Yes Megan?"
"Can Luath sit at the table with us for Xmas dinner?"
"Och Megan can you not count, I've already set a place for him."

"Thanks Mum."

And so as they all sat down at the table and Jock said..
"Let's put our hands together and say a prayer for Our Lord's birthday and for sending Luath back to us."
"Dear Lord"
Jamie and Megan looked at Luath.
Luath was sitting on his back legs with his two front paws up at his nose, as if praying.
"Look at Luath." Said Jamie.
They all burst out laughing, it lasted for two or three minutes, then they calmed down. Maggie looked over at Luath and winked at him with both eyes, and Luath just winked back.

And so after they had their Xmas dinner they went and got Clarinda to go for a wee walk before it got dark. They walked along the auld railway track, and then down the wee path to the Glazert water, where stood the big Redwood Tree.
"Pappa, remember you said that you would take us up the top of the Campsies?" Said Megan.
"Oh yes I certainly will Megan, next summer I'll take yous up tae the Meikle Bin and to Earls Seat the highest point of the Campsies, and I'll tell you all about the 'Field of Blood' and how Rob Roy MacGregor's men were defeated there."
"That will be great Pappa, but Pappa what do you think the reason was that we got Luath back?"
"Your prayers were answered." Said Jock.
"What about Robin Redbreast and the Redwood Tree?" Asked Megan.
"Well I suppose it was a mixture of everything, but most importantly you all had faith, and it worked." Said Jock.
"Don't forget ma letters tae God Pappa." Said Jamie.
Megan and Clarinda smiled at each other.

"Okay kids, it's starting to get dark, and look at they big black clouds over there." Said Jock.
"Watch this Pappa." Shouted Jamie.

Jamie lifted a handful of snow and threw it into the Glazert River and said.

"Or like the snow,
Falling on the river,
One moment white,
Then gone forever".

And so they all started to walk back home. The kids walked on in front of Jock. Jamie held Luath close by his side. There was no way Luath was getting out his sight. Megan and Clarinda walked behind them hand in hand, they were so happy.

'Aye it's been a great day the day.' Thought Jock. 'Let's hope there are many more to come. And then it started to rain as the Crambo Clinkers made their way home along the Crooked Valley in Auld Campsie Toun.

And it smells like rain,
Maybe even thunder,
Wont you keep us from all harm,
Wonderful Redwood Tree?

The End